CW01064925

PRAISE FOR *DIGGER AND ME*

"A wonderful tale, told with heart,
hope and a shiny wet nose."
– Gill Lewis, author of *Swan Song*

"A really special book."
– Hilary McKay, author of *The Skylarks' War*

"A story full of humanity."
– Cath Howe, author of *Ella on the Outside*

"Funny, touching and deeply true, it's a story
about the 'red thread' that binds a family together
through illness and change, and the love of a dog."
– Sinéad O'Hart, author of *The Eye of the North*

"A simply perfect book about a boy and his dog
navigating a painfully well-observed imperfect situation...
Funny and warm and ultimately leaves a glow."
– Perdita Cargill, author of *Waiting for Callback*

"Heartbreakingly brilliant! Warm, funny, sad,
tender, with poetry that punches your heart."
– Tamsin Winter, author of *Being Miss Nobody*

"A gorgeous uplifting story about dogs, step-families
and how they come in all shapes and sizes, and
the difference a great teacher can make."
– Rhian Ivory, author of *The Boy Who Drew the Future*

"Warm, funny, kind, heartbreaking in places, but most
of all just so vivid. It'll stay with me for ages!"
– Nicola Penfold, author of *Where the World Turns Wild*

"The story of a young boy who navigates his way through
the tricky territory of family changes and new relationships
with his beloved pet dog. A masterpiece in observation.
Tender, humorous, important."
– Rachel Delahaye, author of *Mort the Meek*

"A truly lovely book. My heart is thoroughly warmed!"
– Sharon Gosling, author of *The House of Hidden Wonders*

For my agent, Gill McLay –
for your belief in me but more than that,
your belief in every young reader

LITTLE TIGER

An imprint of Little Tiger Press Limited
1 Coda Studios, 189 Munster Road, London SW6 6AW

Imported into the EEA by Penguin Random House Ireland,
Morrison Chambers, 32 Nassau Street, Dublin D02 YH68

www.littletiger.co.uk

A paperback original

First published in Great Britain in 2024
Text copyright © Ros Roberts, 2024
Illustrations copyright © Catherine Fortey, 2024

ISBN: 978-1-78895-676-5

A CIP catalogue record for this book is available from the British Library.

Printed and bound in the UK.

MIX
Paper | Supporting
responsible forestry
FSC® C171272

The Forest Stewardship Council® (FSC®) is a global, not-for-profit organization
dedicated to the promotion of responsible forest management worldwide.
FSC defines standards based on agreed principles for responsible forest
stewardship that are supported by environmental, social, and economic stakeholders.
To learn more, visit www.fsc.org

10 9 8 7 6 5 4 3 2 1

ROS ROBERTS

Knowing the Score

LITTLE TIGER

LONDON

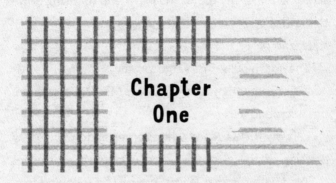

Chapter One

The coach rumbles along the motorway, bringing us closer and closer to home.

Jess nudges me and offers me a sweet. "Look!" she says, and points to a big blue sign for Chester.

I take the mint and smile.

"I can't wait to sleep in my own bed," she says.

I nod. "Me too."

She pops the packet back into the white carrier bag by her feet and twists round to talk to Surinder. The bag topples to one side so I reach down to straighten it.

We each have one, filled with the things we made during the school residential. A clay pot, macramé drink mat, painting of a tree and a large piece of A3 paper with a mind map of special people in our life. I can see the edge of Jess's map. It's covered in names, the words scuttling across the top of the paper and tumbling down the other side, three sisters and fourteen cousins all squeezed on.

The coach pulls off the motorway.

"Start gathering your things," says Miss Dolan over the bus microphone.

I lift my rucksack and white carrier on to my lap. My painting of the giant oak is poking out, the branches dappled with summer leaves. I've tucked the mind map behind it. There's a lot of empty space on mine.

Jess sorts her bags and taps my painting. "Your tree is *so* cool," she says, smoothing down one of the tissue-paper leaves.

"Thanks," I say. I sit back and watch the fields flash by. We pass the farm and turn into the long, steep road up to school. I can see the supermarket where Mum works and the road that leads to our flat. The lady from the launderette is locking the door. The clock on the market archway says six o'clock. Everyone is heading home.

I'm so ready to see Mum.

The coach climbs the hill, passes through the traffic lights and pulls into the school car park. We all start searching for our parents. I spot Mum, standing at the back of the group on a raised bit of grass, her right hand twisting the silver hoops on her necklace, her left holding on to her red sun hat as she searches for me. The coach spins round and reverses and then she spots me. I wave hard and she yells so loudly that the other parents turn round to look.

Chapter Two

"I missed you so much, Gem," says Mum, scooping lasagne on to my plate.

"I know," I say. "Me too."

"What was the *best* thing about the trip?" she says.

I don't feel like talking. I'm tired. But I know she needs to be with me, talk to me. "The kayaking. Surinder fell in."

"Oh!" says Mum. "Poor her."

"Jess thinks she did it on purpose."

Mum laughs and picks up the white carrier bag sitting by the table. "Can I see?" I nod and she pulls out the painting of the tree. She strokes the leaves, follows the line of the branches, pats the strips of real bark on the trunk. "This is beautiful," she says. "Can I frame it?" I nod again and take a piece of garlic bread.

She pulls out the clay pot and the macramé drink mat, examining them. "Gorgeous," she says and then she takes out the special people map and lays it flat on the table, reading the names. She reads the list of friends, topped by Jess and Surinder, of course. And then she looks at the family list. *Me, Mum, Gran, Uncle Jo.* I'm not sure how she'll feel about it. She sniffs a little and moves it to one side, pulls her plate closer and picks up her fork, picking at the edge of the pasta. "Joe has an 'e' on the end of his name. J-O-E."

"Oh," I say. "I didn't know."

She shrugs. "It doesn't matter."

We are quiet while we eat. Mum stops looking at the things in the bag, stops talking, just finishes her dinner. It's like seeing Gran's and Uncle Joe's name on the map has taken her words away. But making the special people map made me think about them more.

"Jess asked me about Uncle Joe and where he lived, and I didn't know what to say."

"Oh," says Mum. "He doesn't live too far away." She moves her plate to one side. "I got some chocolate puds." She twists round and opens the fridge and puts them on the table. "A treat to welcome you home."

"Thanks," I say.

"You should have added Jerry and Sadie to the special people map."

"They're *your* friends, Mum," I say.

"Yes, but they're really like family."

I peel the lid off my pudding and say, very quietly, "They're not." And then I can't help myself. "I just wish…"

"What?" she says.

"Well, I just wish I saw Gran and Uncle Joe a bit more."

She stirs the chocolate. "Oh … well, you *do* see them… It's just … Gran…" I wait while she forms the words. But then she stops, takes a mouthful of pudding and rattles on instead about a difficult customer at the supermarket who moaned about a dodgy pineapple.

Things are tricky between Mum and Gran. They always have been. There was a big fallout years and years ago, after Mum came back from America. I don't know what about. Mum hates talking about those days. I pick up scraps of information, scramble with tiny memories of things. But it's like a jigsaw, all broken up, thousands of pieces that I can't even begin to put together.

I asked her about it once. We had been at the cinema for my birthday, watching a film about a lost dog crossing America. On the bus home, I asked Mum about her trip to America, and what happened when she got home.

She looked at me, gasped a little and then stared out at the dark night and said, "America is a great place." She didn't talk much again that night, even though it was my birthday.

I only see Gran twice a year, at Christmas and near my birthday. We meet at the shops or the cinema or a café. She's funny, Gran; she makes me laugh. We talk about all sorts of things: school, swimming, food. But we never talk about things that matter. We never talk about my mum or the fallout or why we hardly ever see Uncle Joe. It's like we've put all that stuff in a box and shoved it away in a cupboard.

I scrape my chocolate pot clean and clear the table. Mum reaches for me and I hug her hard.

"I'm just going to finish this module," she says, picking up her nursing books. "And then I'll come and help you unpack."

I pick up the white carrier bag and go to my room, lie on my bed and listen to the familiar, wonderful sounds of home. The big double deckers that pass by so close that the windows shake. Mum tapping on her laptop next door. Mrs Dawkins' TV in the flat above ours, the voices so loud I can almost hear what they're saying.

I reach down to the bag and pull out my special

people map. I trace my fingers over the names, reach for a pen and add a neat 'e' to the word Jo.

I might show it to Gran, next time I see her. I'm just not sure when that will be. It's a long time until Christmas or my birthday.

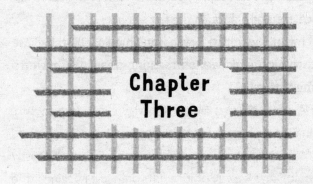

Chapter Three

"I'm sure this hill gets steeper every week," says Mum.

"Or the laundry heavier," I say. We are carrying a bag each, all of it soaking wet, ready to hang out to dry. My hair is wet too. I swim on a Saturday and then we carry the laundry back home together.

"Jaz says I could do with an extra coaching session before the gala," I say. "But we'd need to pay."

Mum hitches the laundry up, puts both hands under the bag. "That's OK," she says. But I know it's not. Mum wanted to use the dryers at the launderette today, but she didn't have enough money and the cash machine wouldn't give her any.

We get home and hang the washing out. Mum's phone rings. It's Jerry on video call. She props him up on the fruit bowl while she hangs up the last things. I go to my room and sort out my swim stuff but I can hear Jerry's voice, shrieking through the flat.

"I won! I won! I've never won anything. Nothing! Me and three friends, a month-long cruise – you have to come, Carrie!"

"A *month*?" says Mum. "No way can I do a month. I can't leave Gemma for that long."

"I'd love Gemma to come too, Carrie, honestly I would," says Jerry. "But it's adults only. Just imagine ... the Caribbean ... for a month ... all paid. We'd leave in about four weeks."

"I can't," says Mum. "However much I'd love to."

I peek my head out of my room, staying out of view. She's sat down now, resting her chin on her hands. Jerry lists off the places they'd visit. Mum winces a little as he talks about Barbados, tosses her head up to look at the ceiling. "I can't get a month off work," she says. "And there's my course deadline."

"That could all be sorted," says Jerry. "You've aced every module of your course so far and that supermarket owes you a favour. They'd collapse without you. And Gemma is growing up. Just imagine it, Carrie. You, me, Sadie and Reuben. Have a think and let me know, soon as you can." He blows her a kiss like he always does, a giant raspberry spluttering through the air, and then ends the call.

I go back to my room to dry my hair. I move the dryer up and down, thinking about Jerry's news. I reach for my special people map and stare at the names. I think about Jess at the residential telling stories about holidays with her cousins, and Surinder describing how she gives up her bedroom for her gran when she comes to stay. I would love Gran to come and stay here, in my room. I'd love Uncle Joe to visit too, and for us to spend time with them, like normal families.

We need to fix this rotten fallout and be a family again.

And I think this cruise might have given us the ideal time to start.

Chapter Four

An hour later, the washing has been rearranged, some on to hangers. The kitchen is super tidy and Mum is cleaning, deep cleaning. She only cleans when something is really bothering her. I grab a duster to help, lift up the candleholders and the brass elephant that sit on our little lounge table. We both smile when we see the dust-free shapes left underneath.

"Been a while since I did this, Gem," she says.

I wipe the surface clean. "I heard Jerry today, on the phone."

Mum turns and looks at me. "Oh, that," she says, wafting her duster in the air, as if to waft the call away, pretend it was nothing. "So great for him."

I wipe the elephant, try to push the yellow cloth into the grooves of his trunk. "You should go."

"I know," I say.

She gives me a little hug and goes to her room and I'm pretty sure we won't talk about it again today.

Chapter Five

On the last Friday of every month, Mum and I have our treat takeout. It's a special night for us. It's Chinese tonight, our favourite five boxes of goodies lined up on the table. We dish sweet and sour on to our plates and just as I'm scooping out some egg fried rice Mum says, "The cruise ship has a Chinese buffet ... according to Jerry."

I look at her, not sure what to say. Mum hasn't said a thing about the trip all week and I haven't asked. She picks up a spring roll, sits up straight and says, "If you'd like to stay with Gran, I think that might be rather nice." She bites the roll, a few beansprouts hanging off her bottom lip. She hooks them back in.

"Do you mean while you go on the cruise?"

She nods, chews, tucks the filling back inside the

half-eaten spring roll. "Gran said she couldn't imagine anything lovelier, and work seems to think I should go. I've even extended my course deadline." She blinks hard and looks at me. "I just don't know if I can leave you, Gem." One hand reaches out to stroke my face.

"It's only four weeks, Mum, and I'd like to spend some time with Gran. I've never even *been* to her house."

Mum nods. "You have, but when you were very young."

"Well, I don't remember. I want to go to Gran's." I scoop out the last of the egg fried rice.

"I suppose you and Gran could have fun together," she says. "You'll love her dogs."

I nod and smile and finish my food. I feel bad that I'm not telling her my main reason for going. To find out about the fallout ... to try to fix things between her and Gran and Uncle Joe. But if I tell her, she'll stop talking, stop being excited, probably not want to go any more. So instead, I just say, "And Mum, you deserve this holiday *so* much."

She bites a prawn cracker and we hold hands for a moment. "You think?" she says, stroking my fingers like she always does.

I nod hard. "Absolutely."

"OK, I'll phone Jerry later, if you're *really* sure?" She looks happier, excited.

"One hundred per cent."

"Can I show you the brochure on my phone?"

"Of course!"

She gets her bag and rummages for her phone and as she pulls it out, a new swimsuit with tags gets caught in the strap. She tucks it back inside. Mum hardly ever buys new things for herself. She shows me the photos and then says we'll call Gran and tell her it's all going ahead.

I've never been with Mum when she's phoned Gran. It sounds odd but it's true. Mum will just say, "Gran is taking you out on Saturday for your birthday," and then it happens.

She scrolls down her contacts and finds *Mum* and it feels strange seeing that. I think about how close me and Mum are, how we do so much together. She hardly ever sees her own mum. She presses call and it rings and rings and then Gran answers and when Mum says I'd love to come, Gran shrieks so loud Mum has to hold the phone away from her ear.

Gran and I chat and make lots of plans. Trips out, the cinema, the zoo, dog walks, baking, seeing Uncle Joe. Mum sits listening, tidying up the takeout cartons and when the call is over, she looks a little unsure again, as if the plan now seems the silliest idea in the world.

"Did I hear you're seeing Joe?" she says, moving to the sink to wash the cartons.

"Yes," I say. "I'm so excited!"

"Mmm," she says and she wipes the cartons hard, rinsing them over and over until they're like new.

"Is that OK?" I ask.

She spins round and smiles.

"Of course! You'll love him, I'm sure." There's something strange about the way she says it. Like she's talking about him in the past, thinking about the way she *used* to know him, many years ago.

Chapter Six

Mum and I walk away from the Year Six leavers' assembly hand in hand. She is crying a little, clutching me as if I might blow away if she doesn't hold on.

"I just can't believe," she says, "that primary school is done!"

I nod and we catch up with Jess and her mum. We compare our shirts, covered in everyone's signatures and messages. We walk together, talking about memories of school and our plans for the summer.

"Wow, Carrie," says Jess's mum. "I hear you're going on a cruise! How exciting! When do you leave?"

Mum stops, blinks a little and says, "Um, I'm not sure."

I stare at her, puzzled. "In four days' time, Mum! We've been counting the days!"

"Yes," she says. She looks away down the street, puts

her hand to her necklace. "That's right."

"I'm so jealous!" says Jess's mum. "Have a great time!" We reach their road and Jess and I do our big goodbye hug.

"Honestly, you two!" says her mum. "You'll be chatting on your phones in five minutes!" We all laugh except Mum who tries to smile, but as they head off she sniffs deeply and looks really upset.

"Are you OK?" I ask. "It is sad, primary school being over, but it's meant to be *me* that's a sniffling wreck, not you!"

She manages a tiny smile but as we carry on down the road and break away from the crowd she stops and looks at me.

"It's not just about today, Gem," she says. She nibbles her bottom lip and hugs her bag to her chest. "Gran had a fall in the night and broke her hip. I got a call just after you left for school."

"Oh no. Is she OK?"

"She's having surgery right about now. I visited her this morning, while she was waiting to go in. She's so cross with herself."

"It's good you went to see her," I say. It's a big thing, Mum going to see Gran.

She nods, stares into the distance.

"I got a call from Joe." She says the words very quietly. "He went in the ambulance with her. He asked me to come."

"I'm glad he was there," I say. "To help Gran."

"Yes," she says.

"Will Gran be OK when I go to hers on Monday?" I ask.

"That's the thing," says Mum. "I'm afraid not. She may even be in hospital still."

"Oh." I feel funny in my tummy. We were both super excited and now the plan is falling apart.

"So the trip's off," says Mum. "I've phoned Jerry and told him I can't go." She flicks her hair back and walks on, faster now, as if she's trying to show me that she's fine about it all. Other kids bump past us, shrieking and excited that the holidays have begun.

I catch up with her, tug her arm, think of her new swimsuit with the tags, the little pile of travel-size holiday bottles on her bed.

"No," I say. "You can't do that."

She turns to look at me, gives me a quick hug . "It's fine, Gem. We can do some nice things together."

I walk beside her, my mind racing, trying to come up with a plan. Surinder is about to go away. Jess is staying with her dad down south for the next few weeks. And then I think of it. The ideal solution.

"Why don't I stay with Joe?"

Mum pulls an "as if that's going to happen" face.

"That won't work," she says. "And I expect Jerry has found someone else by now. He was going to ask a few friends at the volunteer centre. I bet annoying chatty Sally will go instead."

I feel a bit hot, a bit odd. Mum's big suitcase is packed, her passport and documents ready in a plastic folder. I was excited to stay with Gran, see Joe and try to find out about Mum's family. I don't want our plans to fall apart.

"If it was OK for me to stay with Gran," I say, very slowly, trying not to say the wrong thing, "then surely it would be OK for me to stay with Uncle Joe?"

Mum shakes her head. "You hardly know him." She marches on, me stumbling beside her, my thoughts swirling, trying to get the trip back on track.

"Well, no, but I'd *like* to. And I did see him at Gran's birthday lunch ... and I was his bridesmaid, wasn't I?"

"That was a long time ago, Gem. You were five!"

"The lunch was only last year," I say. "Come on, Mum, he *is* my uncle."

"We didn't even speak to him at the lunch," she says.

It's true. We didn't. But that wasn't his fault. Joe had called out, asked us to join him, but Mum had grabbed seats down the other end of the table. We ate the main course and then one of Gran's friends asked Mum about her job and if she'd ever like to go back to America. She got a headache then and we had to leave before pudding or the cake.

We reach our front door. Mum rummages in her bag for her keys.

"So," I say. "Shall we ask Joe if I can stay with him?"

She shakes her head.

"What's the big deal? Is he not very nice or something?"

"Not *nice*?" She laughs and scoffs and says, "*Everyone* loves Joe!" She finds the key and shoves it in the lock, pushes the door hard. "My brother ... the golden boy." She drops her bag to the floor.

I bend down to undo my laces. "*You* don't seem to think he's the golden boy," I say, just quietly but she hears me and spins round, staring at me.

"What happened all those years ago, Mum?" I ask, looking up at her. "What happened to make you *so* cross?"

Her eyes go wide, she reaches for her silver hoops. "Nothing, nothing at all, Gem."

But we both know *that's* not true.

Her phone rings.

"That'll be Jerry," she says, taking her phone from her back pocket. She's relieved, I think, to have the moment broken, to stop my questions. "Probably calling to tell me chatty Sally is going on the cruise." She stares at the screen and pauses for a moment before answering it. "We were just talking about you," she says.

I cross my fingers very hard and hope chatty Sally *hasn't* got a free month's holiday. But it's not Jerry. It's Joe.

At first Mum stands very still and talks like she does to her boss at work. But after a minute she sits down and her voice softens and I'm glad. They talk about Gran and the hospital and the operation and visiting times. And then Mum stops and looks at me and raises her eyebrows.

"Mum told you about that, did she?" she says. "Yes, but it's a month... Yes, but you have to work... You'd do that ... you have leave to take? Funnily enough, Gemma asked if she could stay with you... I'll think about it ... we'd need to meet... OK, I'll call you later..." She hangs up and looks at me with a little smile, as if she can't help herself. "It seems Joe would love to have you to stay. He can take some time off work. What do you think?"

"I think yes!" I say and I throw my arms around her,

the relief flooding through me. My plan is back on track. "Call Jerry *now*!"

She calls him. It's fine. Chatty Sally was off sick with flu.

"Oh, I love the flu!" yells Mum and she hugs me tight. And suddenly the problems fade a little and it's as if the awkward questions about Joe and her have been tucked away again, neatly out of the way, like always.

Gemma: HOLIDAY DRAMA – Gran's broken her hip so now I'm staying with my uncle Joe

Surinder: shame u can't go on the cruise. I'd love to go on a cruise

Jess: 👍

Surinder: ur mum is sooooo lucky!!!!

Jess: bet ur uncles cool

Gemma: I don't even know him!

Surinder: 🙈

Jess: it'll be fab

Gemma: 🤍

Chapter
Seven

The airport tannoy bellows out another announcement. Mum stops and listens, stares at the floor, the clock.

Flight AB235 to New York...

"It's a shame," I say, "that we didn't have that meet-up dinner with Joe."

"I know," says Mum, fiddling with the edge of her kaftan, pulling out loose threads. The kaftan is like a giant cone of swirly carpet. You could hide under it. A whole family could hide under it. "But we had the video call instead. You and Joe got on really well."

I nod and pinch my lips a bit. Mum had hardly spoken on the call, just let Joe do all the talking and I could tell it was hard for him.

"A proper get together would have been better," I say. "It's odd that the supermarket had an emergency that day and we had to cancel."

"Mmmm," she says.

I want to say, "Did someone slip on a banana skin and you had to call an ambulance?" but Mum looks so frantic right now, I know that won't help. I sit down on the airport floor, cross-legged.

Her phone beeps and she grabs it fast, answers the text. "Jerry and the others are at the gate. Where is he? We said right *here*." She looks down at me, strokes my cheek. "You do *know* Joe though, love," says Mum. "From the lunch and the wedding."

It makes me cross she says that. Four days ago, she said I hardly knew him. Now she's trying to convince herself that this is all OK; that I do know Joe and it doesn't matter that we didn't meet up.

"I was five at the wedding," I mutter, looking up at the huge white ceiling. "That's a long time ago."

The wedding. I don't like thinking about the wedding.

"How long did Uncle Joe stay married?" I ask, just to make sure that horrid lady won't be with him today.

"Six months," says Mum, up on tiptoe, scanning the crowds.

"Wow," I say. "She really wasn't very nice."

Mum flicks round fast, looks at me and says,

"It usually takes two, Gemma. Maybe *Joe* wasn't very nice."

I hug my knees tight as she turns back, the kaftan catching on my shoulder. There is a stickiness between us today. Among these thousands of people, there is this odd sticky air between us.

"Well," I say, "if he's not so nice, why are you sending me to stay with him for a month? You said *everyone* loves him."

Mum glares at me and then she sniffs deeply and blinks.

"Joe's fine," she says quietly. She rummages in her bag to check for the tenth time that her tickets and passport are there. "I'm sure you'll adore him like *everyone* else." I look up at her. Stare hard. She squeezes my shoulder. "And you'll see Gran. She's coming out of hospital today."

Passengers for flight AB235 to New York, please head to gate number fifty-four.

The tannoy seems to sound louder and more insistent.

"That's my flight and I haven't even been through security," says Mum, tugging at her hair, and I feel a little sorry for her now. The plan is coming apart.

Which means she might too. And then her eyes lift and her hand waves madly.

"At last!" she shouts and the kaftan jumps up and down.

Chapter Eight

Joe is tall and tanned and is wearing a really cool jacket with buckles on the collar. He gives Mum a hug. She hugs him back which surprises me. I think it's more from relief than sisterly love. He flicks his floppy fringe and smiles at me.

"Thought you'd like these, Gemma," he says, and he passes me a plastic bag full of jelly beans. I jump up and take them and say thanks.

"Oh," says Mum. "Gem isn't really allowed artificial col—"

Joe just raises his eyebrows and says, "Thought you had a flight to catch."

"Yes," says Mum. "I do." She zips her bag tight, strokes my hair, kisses my cheek hard. "Love you so much, Gem."

"Love you too, Mum."

She turns and leaves, one hand pulling her suitcase, jogging in the direction of security. Her foot catches on the kaftan and she trips a little and it suddenly hits me that I won't see her for a whole month. I worry she didn't hear me say that I love her so I shout it, quite loudly, across the airport. A few people nearby hear and look round and smile.

Mum turns and blows me a kiss and then she dashes round the corner to the security gate and is gone.

I stare after her, feeling a little sick in my tummy.

"Right," says Joe. "Let's have some fun. I hope the sweets are OK."

I glance down at my hand holding the bag. I've been clutching it so tight that the jelly beans are all squashed against the plastic.

"Great ... thanks," I say.

Joe picks up my bag. "This all you got?"

"Yep, and this." I twist round so he can see my backpack.

"OK," he says. "This way." And I follow him, running a little to keep up, darting in and out of all the people standing, looking, dashing, crying, laughing, hugging.

"Where's she flying to again?" says Joe, looking back at me over my shoulder.

"New York," I say. "To go on a cruise with Jerry. Who never cuts his hair."

Joe laughs. "What *never*?"

"Nope," I say. "He wears it in one long plait, all the way down his back."

"Bit like Rapunzel," says Joe, and I laugh, very loud. And then I feel bad for laughing about Jerry. He's actually pretty cool.

"He works for the wildlife sanctuary," I say, but as I say it, the tannoy bellows out information about a flight to Dubai and Joe doesn't hear.

We head for the exit and battle our way through the rotating doors and on to the pavement. Joe stops and stares at the car park signs as if he's forgotten where he parked the car.

"Jerry saves otters and foxes," I say.

"Wow," says Joe, but I'm not sure he really knows what I'm talking about. He sets off again and I trot behind.

We get to a silver kiosk and Joe gets out his wallet to pay for the parking. Then he's off in search of his car. I stand back a bit and watch him and try to match him up with the Uncle Joe that got married all those years ago.

Chapter Nine

Uncle Joe's car is small and red. He puts my bag in the boot and we climb in. The engine makes a loud noise as it comes to life and the whole car kind of trembles.

Joe throws his jacket in the back but it catches on my seat belt, so I pull it free and turn round to put it on the tiny back seat. It's covered in tennis rackets and tins of balls. I lay it on top of the mess.

We set off, whizzing up and down the rows of parked cars, looking for the exit. I stare ahead, gazing up at the sky. A plane is lifting high. I wonder if Mum is in it.

"I like the way your car rumbles," I say.

"Thanks, Gem! What sort of car does your mum have?"

"We don't have one."

"Oh," says Joe. He stops at the barrier, shoves his

ticket in the machine and turns to look at me. "What, not at the moment, or at all?"

"At all," I say. The barrier lifts. We drive out and I search the sky for Mum's plane again.

"How do you get around?" asks Joe. He hurtles past a large van and I grab the seat to steady myself. The car feels like it's scraping the ground.

"Um ... buses, trains. We walk a lot. Some of Mum's friends have cars and they take us places."

Joe taps the wheel. "Cool," he says.

I look out of the window and watch the fields and buildings flash by. I'm not sure if it is cool or not. Mum always says we can't afford a car. I'm not even sure if she can drive.

Joe puts some music on. I reach down to my backpack and take out the bag of sweets. The top is all crunched up, so I open it and take out some jelly beans. They are sugary and soft and lovely. I move the bag closer to Joe. "Want some?" He puts his hand in and takes a few.

We join the motorway, the road signs turning big and blue.

"So, a whole month," he says, turning the music down a bit. "You OK with that, Gemma?"

I nod and then I realize he can't see me nod so I say,

"Of course." We come up behind a big lorry. I can read *CLEAN ME* on the back doors. Joe starts to overtake.

"I was really pleased when your mum said you could come and stay," he says, the car speeding up as he puts his foot down and drives alongside the lorry. "Bit shocked she trusted me to take care of you, to be honest."

"*I* was shocked," I say. "To be honest." I glance at the lorry driver. I have to look way up and tilt my head.

Joe laughs out loud and looks at me again, as if he's surprised at what I said. "You've got your mum's quick wit!"

I don't know what that means. But I don't ask.

"I was pleased, though," says Joe. "Gran talks about you all the time."

"Oh," I say. I don't think that's true. There's not a lot to talk about when you only see someone twice a year. "Is Gran OK?"

"She's her normal feisty self again," says Joe. "Determined to be back on her feet as soon as possible. She goes home today, with carers popping in to help. We're going to see her next weekend, at her house. It will be fun, to be together again."

I'm quiet for a moment. I think of Mum, tripping at the airport, crying when we left the flat this morning, the way she tucked a ten-pound note in my hand for the trip.

"We won't all be together," I say. "Mum's not with us."

"No," he says. "That's true. And that's a shame. But I'm sure she'll be having a blast. And I hope, when she's home, we will have more times, you know, the four of us." He glances quickly at me, as if he wants to see if I feel the same.

I nod and say yes.

I like the way Joe said that, about the four of us. It's like he wants to fix things too.

<hr />

It's hard to match up this Joe with the Joe from the wedding. He looks so different. At the wedding, he seemed huge, with a beard and an earring and stripey socks. He had smiled at me and said, "You look beautiful," and I had looked up at him and said, "You look like a pirate," and he had laughed, very loud.

I have a few, clear memories of that day. A pink bathroom with ruffly curtains where Gran tugged me into a flouncy dress, my posy of roses, and the moment in the cold stone church just before we walked down the aisle. The bride was tall with long white hair and a sharp nose and she had leaned towards me in that echoey grey room, pointed her red painted finger and said, "Stay a few paces behind me. Don't trip on my train." And I didn't know what she meant because I couldn't see a train. She was an ugly sister, not a Cinderella bride. I guess Uncle Joe took a bit longer than me to work that out.

The wedding was meant to be a fresh start for us all. I don't know why I know that, but I do. Me a bridesmaid. Mum in a big, flowery hat. But it lasted about as long as the roses I carried down the aisle. I remember all this like you remember things from a dream; odd memories that pop up in your mind but have nothing to link them. Flowers, roses, the pink bathroom, Mum crying, a journey somewhere, the nasty bride. They bump into each other, all those things, but however hard I try, I can't slot them together.

We overtake a huge car transporter. "Not long now," says Joe.

The fields and buildings flash by. I don't recognize anything. We come off the motorway and after a few roundabouts we join a long, straight road, lined with beautiful trees. The leaves meet overhead, making a tunnel.

"This is so pretty," I say. "Mum would love this."

Joe taps his hand on the wheel. "Does your mum still work at the supermarket?"

"Yes," I say. "She runs the fruit and veg bit. We eat a *lot* of fruit and veg. Especially the stuff they have loads of. I am *so* fed up of carrots."

Joe laughs. "I promise I won't give you carrots, the whole time you're with me."

I smile, but I'm worried I've made Mum's job sound silly.

"She's just got a promotion," I tell him. "She's in charge of the staff as well as the fruit and veg now."

Joe nods and says, "I bet the supermarket has never been so well organized and the staff so well looked after."

I nod and say, "Yes, she's bossy at work, I think."

Joe laughs. "She always was."

I turn to look at him. I want to ask more about how she always was. But I can't find the words. I spot the little hole in his left ear. I think that must have been where the earring went, when he looked like a pirate at the wedding.

Chapter Ten

Joe turns off the main road and we drive down a lane into a village. There are tubs with flowers and a little shop with a board outside with pictures of ice cream. I hadn't expected Joe to live somewhere like this.

"Do you work here?" I ask.

"No, I get the train to Manchester, from the station near the level crossing. It's not far."

"Wow," I say. "You can get to Manchester for the day from *here*?" It seems incredible. I've only ever been to Manchester once, to see a pantomime with school.

"Yep," says Joe, laughing. A lot of things I say seem to make Joe laugh. He slows down and pulls on to a driveway in front of a modern house. There are three of them in a row.

"This is me," he says. "Come and meet Lexi."

I feel a little sick. It was fine with Joe in the car but now we are at his house it all feels much more real and Mum seems very far away. I'm hoping Lexi is a dog or a cat but as Joe climbs out, a lady comes out of the front door. She is wearing very tight jeans and high heels. She throws her hands in the air.

"Where have you been?"

"Getting Gemma," says Joe. "You know that."

He shuts the car door and walks over to her.

I can't hear what they say after that but I can tell he's trying to calm her down. Lexi looks at me through the passenger window. She lifts one hand as if it's very heavy and she sort of twists her mouth upwards.

I don't want to get out of the car. It's like the time I went to try out for Surinder's netball team. I had gone with her mum and when we arrived, Surinder had jumped out and the group of tall girls with their swingy ponytails and matching purple tops had looked round at me, all of them staring. I had stayed frozen in my seat, not wanting to move, a bit like now.

Joe beckons me to join them. I open the door, peel myself up from the seat and stand there, feeling completely out of place, my cheeks turning pink.

I open my backpack and pretend I'm looking for something.

"Hi, Jenna," says Lexi.

I smile a tiny smile.

"It's Gemma," says Joe.

"It's lovely to meet you..." she says, giving Joe a sideways glance, "Gemma." She reminds me of a supply teacher at school. All the words sound just the same. "I've heard so much about you."

I nod. I'm not sure what to say.

"Is your mum on the cruise yet?"

"Um ... I don't think so."

"She's so lucky," says Lexi. "We were meant to be away this weekend, weren't we, Joe?"

Whoops, I think that's my fault.

He ignores her, opens the boot to get my bag.

"We'll be late for lunch," says Lexi. "Come on. I need to get Minxie."

Surely Minxie is a cat or a dog.

"We'll join you later," says Joe. His voice is low and kind of snappy.

"OK," says Lexi. She waves her keys in the air. "Lovely to meet you..." I think she's forgotten my name again. "I'll see you later, Joe ... if you can try to make it."

Joe stares at her and nods towards me with a sort of "the poor girl has only just got here" look but Lexi just glares at him and climbs into a black car parked on the road.

Joe watches her go and then I follow him into the house.

"Sorry about that," he says, putting my bag down in the hall.

"Does Lexi live here?"

Joe laughs, very loud. "No!"

I'm pleased about that.

"If you need to meet her, I can stay here on my own. I'll be fine," I say.

"No way," says Joe. He throws his keys on to a table and hangs his jacket up. "I want to show you where everything is and get you settled."

I clutch my backpack tight and look around the hall.

"It must be very odd for you, Gemma, coming to stay with me for a month when we hardly know each other."

I shrug. He's not wrong.

"The sweets were a good start," I say, and he smiles at me again and pulls his hand though his hair and pats my shoulder. He walks towards the back of the house and I follow him. The kitchen is very cool, all shiny metal surfaces. There is a ginger cat, curled up on the bench.

I dump my backpack and stroke the cat over and over and it rolls a little and purrs.

"That's Carrot Cake," says Joe.

I turn to him and say, "What?!"

"He's a rescue, got run over right outside the house. No one claimed him. Cost me a fortune in vet's bills."

Joe puts the kettle on and comes over and tickles him under the chin.

"Waste of space," he says, smiling.

"Why did you call him Carrot Cake?"

"I had friends over and we were eating carrot cake when the accident happened. So that was that."

Carrot Cake stretches a little, his tummy on show.

"He's lovely," I say.

"Waste of space," says Joe again but he's smiling. "Would you like a drink, Gemma?"

"Just water, please."

He pours me a glass and makes himself a cup of tea, then takes me on a tour of the house. Big, squidgy sofas, white shutters at the windows, giant photos of racing cars and bikes. There are signs of Lexi. A flowery box of tissues and a pair of high heels but it's Joe's house all right and I'm glad.

We head up the stairs. He shows me the bathroom with its big, walk-in shower.

I think of Mum and me, kneeling in the bath at home, holding the little shower attachment to wash our hair, fiddling with the taps to get the temperature right. We call it the "arctic desert" shower because it's either scorching hot or freezing cold.

I nod and smile and say, "Cool."

"And this is your room." He opens a door opposite. "I hope it's OK. I didn't have much time to get it ready."

There is a wooden bed with a red and white checked duvet cover and a furry cushion. A fluffy rug and lamp to match. A bedside table with a drawer, some notebooks with a pencil on top.

"This is amazing," I say, looking around.

"All my friend Sophie. I can't take the credit."

I pick up the cushion and look at him. "Thanks."

Joe nods and says, "I'll get your bag and give you a bit of time to unpack. Come down when you're ready. Those are for you." He points to the pile of white towels and then he smiles and says, "It's lovely to have you here."

He leaves and I look around the room again, out of the window, down at the road and think about the car and Carrot Cake and how glad I am that Joe saved him.

And then I think of my bed at home and my duvet cover that's very old and has a faded unicorn on it. I glance up at the sky and find an aeroplane trail, a long, high one and I ache for Mum and wonder what she's doing.

Chapter Eleven

I take one of the towels and head for the bathroom. The landing walls are covered in photos. Uncle Joe in a racing car. Gran and Joe on Christmas Day, holding up a giant turkey. Joe and his dad fishing in the river years ago, way before I was born. I know it's Joe's dad because it says *Like father, like son* on the frame. I stare at the older man, my grandfather, Mum's dad. He died when I was a baby. They all have the same nose. It kind of has a bump in the middle. There are more photos of some friends of Joe's and then one of him with a tennis racket, holding a trophy, a big silver one.

And then I stop quite still, hug the towel a little. There, right in the middle, is me in my bridesmaid dress. I'm staring at the camera, eyes wide, both hands clutching the little bunch of roses that I had carried down the aisle.

Mum is beside me in her big, flowery hat, her hand on my shoulder. She looks younger but tired, her mouth a straight line, her head tilted as if this makes up for not smiling. Her right hand is up at her neck and although I can't see clearly, I'm certain she is twisting the little silver hoops on her necklace.

The photo is just me and Mum but behind us is the big house where I got ready. It's like the moment is grabbing me, pulling me back. Purple flowers climb up the back wall of the house and over the door. I had forgotten about those flowers but now, seeing the photo, I remember Gran that day gently holding a clump, telling me to bury my face in them. They smelt wonderful. They were a deep purple, rich and gorgeous. The faded photo shows nothing of that. The flowers are tired and dull, like my memories of that day.

I look at the house, at the windows, try to find the pink bathroom with the ruffly curtains where I got dressed. But there is nothing there to see. Just lots and lots of windows, and the flowers, climbing high across the wall.

Chapter Twelve

When I get downstairs, Joe has laid out a pile of sandwich things.

"What about your lunch with Lexi?" I ask.

"I've said we can't make it."

"Oh, OK. I'm sorry."

"One hundred per cent fine, Gem. Dig in." He points at the food, and I reach for a roll, spread mayonnaise on the bread, add some ham. "You must tell me your favourite things to eat."

"I like all the things Mum doesn't let me eat."

Joe laughs, very loud. "OK," he says. "You'll have to let me be the bad uncle and buy you all that naughty food!" I grin and nod. "And Gem, just to say, call me Joe, don't worry about the uncle bit. Much easier. Don't want you worrying about that stuff."

I'm glad Joe said that but I'm not sure now if I should say, "And it's fine to call me Gem," but I don't.

Joe makes himself a sandwich and we sit down on bar stools at the kitchen island. He looks at me and opens his crisps. "Your mum's done a great job raising you," he says.

I'm not sure what to say, so I just bite my sandwich.

"You know, manners and everything," says Joe as if he wants to lighten it, not make it about all the big stuff.

A big gloop of mayo falls out of my sandwich as I bite into it.

"Maybe I spoke too soon," he says and we both laugh.

"I'm sorry you didn't get to have lunch with Lexi and … Minnie, was it?" I say.

"Minxie," says Joe. "She's Lexi's daughter."

"Oh, is that her real name?"

"No." Joe stops and looks around, stares at the floor. "You know what? I'm not even sure what her real name is. But apparently she was such a minx when she was little, they called her that and it just stuck. She's not changed much. Still a right minx, if you ask me."

Joe picks up the cheese and ham and puts them back in the fridge. "She's just turned thirteen," he says. "Bit like you, Gemma."

"I'm eleven. Twelve in six months."

"Oh yes, of course."

"I'm getting a phone, when I'm twelve, for my birthday."

Joe smiles and puts his things in the dishwasher, so I do the same. It seems odd putting a glass in the dishwasher when it's just had water in it. Mum and I don't have a dishwasher. We have a small silver sink with pink cupboards above it where the plates and cups live.

"Don't you have a phone now?" asks Joe.

"Yeah," I say and I take my phone out of my pocket to show him. It doesn't really have a screen. It has a mess of scratches. "It's Mum's old one. The battery runs out quite fast but it's fine."

Joe leans closer and looks at it. "Hope you don't mind, Gem, but I might need to get you something new to use while you're here. You'll be out all day and I'll need to know I can get hold of you."

"Oh, it'll be fine," I say. "Honestly. Mum's saving hard for this one we've seen and..." I stop, quite suddenly. It doesn't feel right, me saying Mum's saving hard. I get the feeling Joe doesn't have to save hard for things.

Joe just says, "Of course," as if he gets it and points to the laptop sitting on the counter. "Feel free to use that for anything you need." I smile and touch the silver pad. It jumps to life, sleek and quick.

"Can I ask you something?" I say.

"Anything." He reaches up to a cupboard and gets a packet of biscuits, shakes a few on to a plate.

"What will I do when you're at work? You said I'll be out all day. Am I coming with you?"

"Well, I wanted to talk to you about that." Joe smiles, and suddenly I see Mum, so clearly. They smile in the same way. One side lifts more than the other. Like it's a bit wonky. "I've taken the last two weeks off. Thought we could do some sightseeing in Chester; go to the zoo, stuff like that. Maybe even go to London."

I raise my eyebrows. Wow, Joe is really taking this uncle stuff seriously. I take a biscuit, bite into the big, oaty chocolate chunks.

"But I do have to work for the first half of your stay," he says. "So I've booked you into this great tennis camp for those two weeks. I hope that sounds like fun. You play each day and then there's a little tournament at the end. It's only down the road and my friend Sophie can pick you up if I can't collect you, and take you back to hers. Her son Bradley is playing too."

I stop chewing. The biscuit goes into a ball. I persuade my mouth to swallow it and put the rest of it down.

"Tennis?" I say. "I've never played tennis before."

"Oh," says Joe. "I kind of thought you might have at um ... school... Oh."

I stare at Joe, hoping he hasn't actually booked it, paid for it, that maybe he is joking.

"Um," he says, "I can cancel it."

"No," I say. "It's fine."

I feel sick. Like, really sick. I went to a gymnastics camp one summer and it was the worst thing ever. Everyone could do walkovers and vaults and I couldn't even do a backward roll. A few of the girls laughed at me, little sniggers whenever I tried something new. It was even worse than the netball trials.

I break the leftover biscuit in two and tidy up the loose crumbs.

"You've *never* played?" says Joe, tilting his head, pulling his hand through his floppy hair. I really don't know what the big deal is.

"Nope," I say.

"Any ball sports?"

"Not really. Bit of netball. I can swim like a fish, though. Is there a swimming camp?"

He smiles and shakes his head and says, "Don't think so."

I don't want to go but I really don't have much choice

– Joe has booked this tennis thing, paid for it, made plans. He has to work. He thought it was a great idea.

"I'm sure it will be fun," I say. The words come out dry and a bit whispery so I force a smile.

"Minxie will be there," says Joe.

I've never met the girl but something tells me it will now be *less* fun.

"Great," I say.

"And you'll really like my friend Sophie."

I nod. At least I don't have to go home with Lexi.

Joe and I are a bit quiet now, a bit ruffled. It suddenly seems odd sitting in this house that I don't know with this uncle I don't know about to spend two weeks playing a sport I know nothing about.

He finishes his biscuit. "Do you have trainers?"

I shake my head and lift my feet. "Just these," and I show him my cloth mules.

"Shorts? T-shirts?"

"Denim shorts and a couple of T-shirts."

Joe looks at his watch. "I think, Gem, that we need to go shopping."

"Really?" I say.

He nods and smiles. "I need to send a few emails, change a few things around so I can take you to the club tomorrow morning. But then we'll go. Catch the shop before it closes."

I stroke Carrot Cake. "I'm a bit of a problem, aren't I?"

Joe pats me on the shoulder. "The kind of problem I like, Gem," he says. "Not like that waste of space."

I laugh and tickle Carrot under the chin and Joe goes to his office. He leaves the laptop right there so I touch it and search the word "tennis". There is stuff on tournaments and kit and then one of those "People also ask" sections and one question is *Is tennis a hard sport?* The answer is *Many people consider tennis one of the hardest sports to learn.* I close the screen fast and feel a little sick in my tummy.

Gemma: Anyone played tennis? I've got to do a TWO WEEK COURSE!!!!! So nervous.

Jess: I did – it was hard. u have to run a LOT – U WILL BE GREAT!!!

Surinder: no never. I have a revolting verruca. must have been that river on the trip.

Jess: aww poor u. put stuff on it.

Gemma: it wont have been the river

Surinder: hows the uncle

Gemma: cool. he has a cat called Carrot Cake

Jess: cuuute 🌀

Chapter Thirteen

We speed back on to the motorway. The late-afternoon sun is still hot, glowing across the fields.

"You've never played tennis at the park?" says Joe. "Or on the beach with wooden bats?"

Wow, Joe has a real thing with this.

"Nope."

"Badminton?"

"Is that the one where you hit the squidgy triangle thing?"

"Yep."

"I played that with Jerry once, when we were on holiday."

"Jerry with the hair?"

"Yep. And the rescue animals."

Joe nods and says, "Is he your mum's boyfriend?"

"No!" I shout.

"OK!" says Joe. "Just sounds like he's around a lot."

"Mum has a lot of friends who are around a lot."

Joe laughs, very loud. His phone beeps and a name flashes on a screen in front of us. It's Lexi.

"Hope you don't mind," says Joe. "I've said we'll pop over for dinner later. You can meet Minxie before tennis."

"OK," I say. I don't really want to meet them later. I'd like to spend time with Carrot and Joe and get used to my room. That feels enough new for today.

We turn off and after a little bit Joe pulls into a big shopping centre. We get out and head for the sports shop. I follow Joe like I followed him in the airport, trotting behind. He heads for a rack of trainers and asks the assistant to help us. I look at all the price labels. It makes me hot and sweaty.

"These are best for the astro courts," says the guy. "What size?"

"Um, four," I say. I've no idea if I'm still a four. It's been ages since I had new shoes. He goes away to find size four.

Joe has moved on to rackets. "Let's get you a blinder!" he says and he reaches down a black racket and tests it out, bouncing the strings off his wrist.

"Try this," he says. I take it. "OK, um, try to wrap your hand around like this." He moves my hand and I grip the handle. A different assistant comes over and Joe and the lady talk about the best racket for me at my age and size and experience. The trainers arrive. I sit down and slide off my mules. My big toes are sticking out of the holes in my socks.

"Socks?" says Joe and the assistant nods and grabs a pack of white socks from the stand. It's hard to get the trainers on. I'm not a size four. We measure my feet, try on two other pairs. It's hot work. My armpits are damp with sweat.

"OK, clothes!" says Joe when we've at last found the right trainers. "Any preference on colour or style?"

I shake my head.

I follow Joe and the lady round the store. She finds me a tracksuit and two T-shirts and a thing called a skort that is half skirt, half shorts. Joe is smiling. He's loving this. But I'm suddenly really not great. I'm hot and I hate all this shopping and I'm worried I'll hate tennis. I want Mum to be here, guiding me away from all the expensive gear, digging in the bargain bucket to find the reduced stuff. I can feel tears brewing.

We wait in the queue to pay. I rummage in my pocket,

pretend to be looking for something. I squeeze my eyes hard but I can't stop one big fat tear from falling. I wipe it fast, hope Joe hasn't seen. But he has. He leans closer, searches for my eyes.

"Gemma! What is it?" We leave the queue and he guides me to a quiet part of the store.

"It's too much money," I say, choking back the tears.

"Oh, Gem, don't worry about that."

I take a breath, search for a tissue. Incredibly, I have one in my pocket, nestled next to the ten-pound note Mum gave me this morning. I hold the money up for Joe.

"Please take this towards it all," I say. But he shakes his head.

"No way. Keep that for when we do the fun stuff in a couple of weeks. For a souvenir." I shove it back in my pocket. We sit down on one of the benches near the trainers.

Joe leans forward, pulls his hands through his hair, looks sideways at me. "Maybe I've messed up here. I can cancel the tennis. Sorry, I should have talked it through with you first. I just thought it would be fun. And don't worry about the stuff. It's just ... I've missed buying you things over the years."

I'm very still, not sure what to say.

We sit for a moment and then Joe's phone rings. He pulls it free.

"It's your mum," he says. He says hi and passes it over to me. I don't want to talk to her. I'll probably cry more and I don't want her hearing me upset. She won't cope with that. But I haven't any choice.

"Hi, Mum," I say, biting my lip to stop any more tears coming.

"Gem. Hi, love. How are you? I'm missing you SO much. Just wanted to let you know that we've landed in New York."

"Great. Mum... I'm..."

"Ooh, wait a minute, Gem..." She yells to someone that she won't be long. "Sorry, Gem, what was that?"

Joe is folding the gear back up, straightening the tracksuit sleeve where it got turned inside out.

"Um ... nothing, Mum. I'm fine." Joe stands up and signals to an assistant. "It's just..." But Mum doesn't hear me.

"The flight was good," she says. "I watched the best movie and we're out tonight before the ship leaves tomorrow. Everything OK with you guys?"

I watch Joe pass over the basket of gear, hear him say it all needs to go back.

"Yeah, Mum, all good."

"What's your plan?"

"Well, Joe has signed me up..." But then Mum shouts that her suitcase is right there and yes of course she wants to see the Statue of Liberty.

"Sounds great, love. Gotta go, Gem, but I'll call tomorrow. Love you!"

"Yeah. Me too." And she is gone. I press the end button on Joe's screen and I smile a little. His wallpaper is Carrot Cake, curled up on a cushion, one paw over his nose.

"Everything OK?" says Joe, coming back over.

I stand up, nod, sniff hard, pass him back his phone. I think about Joe and how he has to work and how kind he has been. I'll be a real problem to him if I don't go.

"I think I'd like to try the tennis thing."

"You sure?" says Joe.

"Yep," I say, shoving the soggy tissue into my pocket.

He looks at me, tilts his head a little.

"What made you change your mind?"

"Not sure. I saw the picture of Carrot Cake on your phone. He survived a car crash. How hard can tennis be?"

"Wow, that cat has done something useful *at last*!" We both smile and then he says, "Are you really sure,

71

Gem?" and I nod and we race over to the assistant and grab the basket back, laughing as Joe trips over a big wire cage of footballs.

We stand in the queue again.

"I'm proud of you," says Joe and he wraps his arm around me and his buckles catch my cheek. "Takes guts to try new things."

I nod and smile. Mum said the same thing the first morning of gym camp.

We shuffle forward and soon we are at the till and I wince as the guy scans the barcodes and the number on the screen gets bigger and bigger.

I reach for the trainers, the last thing to be scanned. "Please put them back," I say. "I can just play in these." I point down at my mules.

"You think?" says Joe and he takes them from me and passes them to the assistant.

Everything is loaded into a giant white carrier bag, the racket handle sticking out of the top. We walk out of the shop, head back to the car, put the bag in the boot.

"Give it two days," he says. "And if you hate it, then we'll rethink the plan, look for a swimming pool. Deal?"

"Yep!" I say. The deal makes me feel a bit better.

Joe shuts the boot. "It's great to spend time with you, Gemma. I've found it hard not being able to see you much."

I nod and think of my special people map. "Me too."

"And you know what?" says Joe. "Because of that, I'm a big fan of cruise-ship-holiday-winning, badminton-playing, long-haired, animal-saving, boyfriend Jerry!"

"He's *not* her boyfriend!"

"Oh, he so is!" says Joe and we both laugh, very loud.

I'm glad Joe said that thing about finding it hard not seeing me. I think he wants to mend things, just like me.

I skip round to get into the front seat and I'm suddenly aware how small my mules feel. A whole size too small.

Chapter Fourteen

The sun is lower in the sky, a golden ball of summer. We drive back on to the main road, Joe's music playing.

"Was your mum OK?" says Joe, tapping his hand on the steering wheel.

"Yes, fine. Loud as always."

"She was always loud! Especially when she didn't get her way."

I nod and smile and I think about Mum "getting her way". I never think of her like that. We just sort of bumble along, me and Mum, throwing life together. She said that to me once. *You and me, Gem*, she said. *We bumble along, don't we? I like it that way.*

I want to ask Joe so many things but I'm not sure where to start. I want to ask him about the fallout and why he hasn't seen Mum for such a long time. I want to ask what Mum was like when she was younger, what life was like when they were little.

The words are queued up but before I can work out how to ask, Joe says, "Tell me about your mum." I glance at him and then I look back at the road and the words come really easily.

I tell Joe about the trips we go on and how she checks the oven is off thirty times a day and how she lets me buy a new book every month, even if I know she hasn't got the money. I tell him things I've never told anyone before. How she studies late at night, taking courses so she can become a nurse. How she takes all the extra shifts she can at the supermarket and how she sews her own clothes.

"You saw the famous kaftan at the airport," I say and Joe laughs.

"She always liked wearing unusual stuff, especially boots," he says, smiling. "When she was about fourteen, she had a pair of huge, furry boots, like a yeti!"

"Wow, I'd love to see those!"

We both sit staring at the road, thinking about Mum. It's like each of us knows one half of her. Before the big fallout and after.

I start to tell Joe more things but I stop. It doesn't

feel quite right to tell him that sometimes the cashpoint won't give us cash or that I know she has a pot under her bed for putting aside money for our last Friday of the month takeout meal. Or how she wakes me by stroking my hair and how she comes in at night when she thinks I'm asleep and nestles into my neck and kisses me.

"Your mum and I used to have such fun times," says Joe. "She could make me laugh like no one else." He sniffs a little, grips the wheel. "And I could drive her round the bend. Sometimes I would do this thing where I'd not let her go upstairs." He starts giggling. "I would just block her, for ages. I think two hours was the longest time." He tips his head back and sighs. "Good times."

I smile. "How old was she then?"

"Ooh, I don't know. Twelve or thirteen. I'd have been ten. That sort of age."

"So you were super close back then?"

He glances at me. "Very," he says. He looks out at the road, sprays the windscreen to clean it. I wait a bit, want him to keep talking. But he doesn't.

"It seems a shame," I say. "That you're not so close now."

He's quiet for a moment and then he says, "Yes, but she has trusted me with her most precious thing in the world so she must still like me a *tiny* bit."

I smile and grab the chance to dig a bit more. "Mum's never told me what went on," I say. "We've never talked about it."

"It's complicated."

I wait, hoping he will say more. But he just turns the music up, looks out of the window and after a few minutes he points to a church on the hillside.

"That's where we go at Christmas," he says. "It's an ancient chapel, only lit by candles. Gran loves it." The church is like something from a fairy tale, nestled in woodland.

"It's pretty," I say. "I'd like to go one year."

We are quiet because I think we both know that probably won't happen.

Lexi rings. Joe puts it on speaker.

"Where *on earth* are you?" she says.

"Five minutes away," says Joe.

"Well, hurry up, poor Minxie is faint with hunger."

Joe presses a button and Lexi is gone and I'm glad.

Chapter
Fifteen

Lexi's house is a surprise. An old cottage with a door so low Joe has to bend down to go through. We follow her into the kitchen, her high heels tapping across the stone floor. I don't like the noise they make.

She takes a can of Coke out of the fridge and passes it to me. There are pizza boxes piled on the counter and a delicious smell in the air.

"I love your cottage," I say.

"Really?" says Lexi. "I hate it. I'm trying to buy something on the new estate."

I fiddle with the ring pull.

Minxie walks in on her phone, her mouth throwing out words.

"No way ... no way ... she does that again ... OMG, she'll have me to deal with. OK. Laters." She shoves the phone into her back pocket. It sticks out of the glittery denim. She pulls the fridge door open and stares at the shelves. She doesn't look "faint with hunger" to me.

The oven pings. Lexi has gone to the loo so I help Joe to get the pizzas out, both of us chipping at the dough that is stuck to the wire shelf.

"We never have *any* decent drinks," says Minxie. She swings the open fridge door back and forth, like she's gathering pace to slam it. Her hair runs down her back in layers of long golden curls. Nothing like Jerry's. And nothing like mine.

I hold out my can of Coke. "Do you want this?" I say. But she doesn't hear me and she finds a can of her own.

"Come and eat, Minxie," says Joe.

She shuts the fridge door and walks over to the table, throws herself on to a seat.

"This is Gemma," says Joe.

Minxie raises her eyes and says, "Hi," and I say hi back.

Joe cuts up the pizza and we take slices. Lexi joins us, sitting as close to Joe as she can get.

"You looking forward to tomorrow, Minxie?" asks Joe. "Gemma's coming too."

"Uh-huh," she says, pulling long cheese threads from her pizza, stretching them high. "Do you mean, do I *want* to go? NO. It's *so* boring." She rolls her eyes and then slants them over at me as if to make sure I've seen. "I've gone every year for the last three years and I literally get *so* bored."

My pizza is suddenly hard to chew, like it's made of rubber.

Minxie has been playing for years.

"Why did you agree to go again then, Minx?" asks Lexi.

Minxie turns on her mum, eyes glaring. "Because it means the world to Dad and *I* wouldn't do anything to upset him."

I glance from one to the other.

Lexi is staring at Minxie. She pulls away from Joe a little and wipes her hands on a serviette. "Enough of that," she says.

"*What?*" snaps Minxie. "Do you expect me to just ignore him like you do? I bet you don't ignore *your* dad, do you, Gemma?" The words rush out of her mouth and she slumps down, picks at her fingernails.

I pick at the crust of pizza on my plate. I've no idea what to say. No one ever mentions my dad. Ever. I know *nothing* about him. Joe is glaring at her. Lexi cuts up more slices of pizza. The air is very sticky, very odd. It feels like I should say *something*. "I don't..." I mutter in a quiet voice but Minxie isn't listening. She just starts talking again.

"Dad's bought me all this new gear. That brilliant Swedish girl wears it. What's it called? Joe, you must know."

Joe shakes his head, takes another slice of pizza.

"It's the *most* expensive brand," says Minxie.

"Gemma," says Lexi, turning to look straight at me, a forced smile on her lips. "Are you ready to play?"

I nod. I'm so happy to be off the dad thing. I think Lexi means gear so I start to say, "Yes, Joe took me to buy..."

But Joe stops me and says, "Gemma's excited to give it a go. She's not played before."

Minxie puts her pizza down and stares at me. "You've *never* played before?"

I shake my head. Wow, her too. Why is it so odd I've never played tennis? I don't think *any* of my friends play. But I'd rather talk about me not playing tennis than me not knowing my dad.

"You are *so* lucky!" mutters Minxie.

We are quiet for a moment and then Joe says, "If you hate tennis that much, you need to tell your dad not to sign you up. Someone else could have had the place."

Minxie sits forward, takes a sip from her can. "I would

never do that. He pays for the best coaches and kit and he told Pam that I *must* have more help this year to sort my serve out." She tosses her hair, uses both hands to work it into one long, twisted curl.

Sort her serve out.

I don't even know what a serve is.

Minxie starts giggling. "We mess around a lot. Last year we hit the balls over the netting on purpose. Pam went wappy when she worked out what we were doing." She laughs out loud, remembering. "Her face turned bright red, like a tomato. We said..." she spurts Coke on the table, "that if you squeezed her, ketchup would come out of her ears."

Lexi is trying not to smile, wiping her mouth with her serviette.

I feel a bit sick. I wonder who she means by "we". Are there a bunch of Minxies at this tennis camp, all super good and kitted out in top gear, saying "laters" to each other?

"Pam is a great coach," says Joe. "You need to have more respect, Minxie."

She stares at him, her smile wiped away. She looks down at her plate, her face all sour, and picks bits off the pizza crust. "You can't say stuff like that to me."

Everyone is quiet.

And then Joe says, "I can and I will."

I sip my water, fold my serviette.

"I forgot the cucumber and carrot sticks," says Lexi.

She gets up and fetches a bowl from the side and puts it on the table. Joe and I look at each other and smile.

"What?" says Lexi. "What's so funny?" She smiles back at first, as if she's glad the moment has taken the awkwardness of before away.

"Nothing," says Joe. "Just something between me and Gemma."

Lexi doesn't like that. She looks a bit annoyed then, as if we were laughing at her. The odd atmosphere returns.

I lean forward and take a carrot. It's good to have something to do. It tastes different to the carrots at home. At least those crunch. These taste like wet cardboard.

Chapter Sixteen

I can't sleep. The bed is cosy but it's all so different. I'm nervous about tomorrow, worried I'll be dreadful at tennis and everyone will laugh at me. And the dad thing is stuck in my mind, the way Minxie asked about him.

I open the drawer next to my bed and pull out my book. My special people map is folded up inside. I open it and stare at the big, empty space where I might have written the word "dad".

Mum has never talked about my dad. Ever. Neither have her friends or Gran.

I never think about him. I don't know why. It's never mattered.

My phone flashes a message. I grab it, hoping it's Mum. But it's the girls.

Surinder: cant sleep with this verruca

Gemma: they don't keep u awake!

Surinder: this one does – will it spread everywhere?

Jess: no silly. Btw hows the cat gem

Gemma: super cute

Jess: ur so lucky

Gemma: hows ur dads puppy?

Jess: omg adorable. follows me everywhere. I'll send a photo.

Surinder: Does he poo everywhere?

Jess: On mats. he's so cuuuuuute.

Gemma: 🖤 I have to play tennis tomorrow. I'm so nervous.

Surinder: I'd rather play tennis than have a verruca

Jess: 🚫

Gemma: worried I'll look really stupid. Remember how bad I was at netball Sinda? 😵

Surinder: I do! LOL.

Jess: You'll be fab Gem

Gemma: 🖤

I try to read my book but I can't follow the story. The words just seem busy tonight, like my thoughts. I turn off the light and close my eyes.

The bag of tennis stuff is by my bed, the tags still on.

The moonlight is shining on the white carrier, the tip of the racket handle gleaming like silver. I think of Minxie's fancy kit and her "serve", whatever that is. I can hear her voice now. *The new kid … omg it was the funniest…* It'll go like that, I'm sure of it.

A car passes by on the road. I'm glad Carrot Cake is curled up safe downstairs.

I'm here for a whole month. Thirty days. I sit up a little and reach for the notepad and pencil that Joe left on the bedside table. I flick the bedside light back on and open the cover and on the first page I write *days to go* and make thirty in tally lines. Six sets of five. Then I put a line underneath and write "days done" and I put one line. There seems a lot of lines to go. A lot of days and nights.

Joe comes upstairs and uses the bathroom. I flick the light off. I can tell he stops at my door to listen, to check I'm OK, and I feel bad now for making the lines. I flick the cover back in place and put the pad in the drawer and lie back again and listen for cars, but the night is completely still and quiet.

I wonder what Mum's doing in New York. Maybe she's looking up at the Statue of Liberty.

I get out of bed and head to the loo. On the way back, I stop at the wall of photos. The moonlight is strong on the landing. My eyes are used to the dark and I stare at the one of me and Mum at the house with the purple flowers. I want to peel the walls back, find the pink bathroom with the ruffly curtains.

"You OK?" calls Joe, from his room. I call back that I'm fine and I head back to bed and think about Mum and how tomorrow she will board a giant ship and sail away on a vast ocean, and she will be further and further away from me.

Chapter Seventeen

It's a short drive to the tennis club. I feel properly sick, as if the pastry I had for breakfast is waiting to come back up. Joe is in a suit and tie. I liked the jacket with the buckles more.

He pulls up to a small car park. There is a big cage with a green floor, white lines and two long nets.

"There are two courts," says Joe. "And that's the clubhouse." He points at a wooden building with a deck. It has a covered bit with benches underneath.

"Oh," I say and I undo my seat belt and fiddle with the tracksuit zip. I feel so odd in all the new gear.

We are the first to arrive. I sit very still, hoping it's cancelled or Joe got the week wrong or it will pour down and we won't be able to play.

A few other cars pull up.

"Come on then," says Joe.

"Mmm," I say, reaching for my bag and my racket.

"I expect you're nervous," says Joe.

"A bit," I say.

I get out slowly and pull my tracksuit top down and the bottoms up.

A lady waves and comes over. She has soft blonde hair, sunglasses hooked on her head and a T-shirt that says *I love cats*. She has loads of tins of tennis balls in a big net bag.

"Gemma," says Joe. "This is my friend Sophie."

Sophie comes right up to me and hugs me. "Gemma!" she says. "We are so excited to meet you, aren't we, Bradley?" She looks over to her son. He lifts his head and gives the tiniest of nods.

"So," says Joe. "You OK to pick up Gemma today?"

"*OK?*" says Sophie, beaming at me. "I literally *can't* wait. A girl in the house *at last*!"

"Great," says Joe. "I hope you like cats, Gem. You'll be tripping over them."

"I like Carrot Cake," I say.

They both smile. A big black car steams into the car park. I can see Minxie in the front seat, giant headphones clamped on her head. A man in a dark suit gets out, strides over to the clubhouse, calls out Pam's name.

"Right, I'm off!" says Joe, smiling at Sophie. "Don't think me and Geoff have much to say to each other." I think Geoff must be Minxie's dad.

Joe checks I have everything I need and then he wraps his arm around me and gives me a hug. He smells really great. All shower fresh. Then he drives away, waving out of the window. And it's odd because I don't want him to go. I hardly even knew him this time yesterday. And now I'm standing in this car park, feeling a bit alone without him.

Sophie joins me. "Come and meet Coach Pam," she says and I walk with her to the clubhouse. She chats about tennis and the weather and how she's excited I'm here. She's so warm and lovely that my nerves settle a little.

The clubhouse floorboards creak as we go in. There is a long table down the middle with benches either side, a small kitchen and a door labelled *Toilets and Changing Rooms*. Sophie lines up the tins of balls, starts opening a few of them.

Geoff is waiting by the kitchen, arms folded, shaking his car keys in one hand. A lady with a clipboard comes out of the loo. I think this must be Pam. Geoff moves forward and starts talking very fast at her. She is so tiny next to him that she has to tilt her head to look up at him. He's talking as if Pam has done something wrong which seems odd as we haven't even *started* yet.

I feel a bit stupid just standing there so I glance around and look at the notice board. There are photos of the summer tournament winners. Joe is there, holding a trophy.

Minxie walks in, headphones still on her head. Her eyes find me but she doesn't say hi, she just looks me up and down. She is wearing the softest pink fleece. I wonder what she thinks of my navy tracksuit. She sits down on the bench and gets out her phone. I look out of the little window. Bradley is outside, bouncing the ball on his racket, over and over.

"No promises, Geoff," says Pam, quite loudly. "Now I need to get on. This isn't just Minxie's tennis camp."

Geoff turns and walks out of the clubhouse, striding away, shaking his head.

Pam looks down at her list of names. She turns to me and smiles and says, "Hello there, what's your name?"

"Gemma," I say.

"This is Joe's niece," says Sophie.

"Oh!" says Pam. "Oh ... you're *Gemma*! We've been

so excited to meet you, Gemma. How *lovely* you are joining us." She stares at me for a moment, smiles.

I nod and hug my racket and my bag and feel a bit sick. I don't know why they are excited to meet me. I'm *really* not that special.

She ticks me off on her clipboard and then looks up at me and says, "How much tennis do you play, Gemma?"

"Um ... I've never played before," I say.

"Oh," says Pam and she looks at me and then at Sophie and back at me again. "OK, well, I'm sure you'll have fun over the next two weeks. Don't worry! There are a few beginners on the course."

She turns away and I take in a silent breath of relief. It floods through me. They say that in books. That relief can flood through you and now I know what it means. It starts in the middle of you, sort of near your tummy, and then it flows out to every part of you until your fingertips feel it.

Minxie is watching me, tapping her phone on the table, nibbling her fingers on the other hand. I smile a little but she just looks away.

I look out of the window and try to spot beginners. What does a beginner look like? Like me? Bradley doesn't look like one.

Maybe everyone thinks Joe has taught me to play. Maybe they think Joe has taught me tennis and taken me to the cinema and rushed to my birthday parties, arriving late with a big present.

I wish those things had happened.

Chapter Eighteen

Sophie leaves and we head outside to the big wire cage. The ground feels a bit like carpet. There are signs that say *Court One* and *Court Two* and two benches for our gear to go on. Minxie sits down and looks around her, as if she is waiting for a bus.

A girl with a ponytail is hitting a ball against a long wall that sits at one side of the second court. Bang, bang goes the ball. She hits it hard, over and over. She is *definitely* not a beginner. Bradley joins her and they take it in turns to hit. My nerves bubble up again. They *both* know how to hit the ball.

A car pulls up and the doors fly open and two boys race towards the cage. They are identical. Completely the same. They get to the door side by side and fight to be the first through.

So, there is me, bang bang girl, Minxie, Bradley and the twins. Close up they are even more alike, the same as two Cheerios. Nothing to tell them apart.

"Played much, boys?" asks Pam.

"A bit," says one.

"Not much," says the other.

"Yes, we have."

"No, we haven't." One kicks the other and they lean into each other, bending down, ankles flying.

Pam stares at them, puts down her clipboard and gently moves them apart. "Gemma," she says. "Meet Finlay and Max." I'm about to say hi but they run off, chasing each other until they fly into the netting.

Another boy runs on court.

"You must be Raj?" says Pam and she ticks him off her list. "Played much, Raj?"

"I've played a *lot*," he says.

"Good," she says. And then just as Pam is about to start, one more girl arrives. Well, she is pushed in by a lady with a massive skirt and piled-up hair.

"Here she is, Coach Pam!" says the lady, laughing. The girl is reading, the book gripped in both hands, knuckles white. The lady snatches it out of her hands and says, "I'll take that."

"Mum," the girl shrieks. "I'll need that at lunchtime." But her mum ignores her, shoves a racket into her hand and runs out of the court.

"Have fun!" she calls. "See you at two!"

Pam picks up her clipboard again. "And you must be Flori."

Flori nods and pushes her headband back up and looks over at her mum's departing car with such a look of spite that it makes me smile a bit. She looks like one of those kid witches on TV who can set things on fire or make lightning strike.

We warm up with running drills. The twins race off and fall over each other. Minxie says her right foot is sore and she can't run. We do some throwing and catching drills and then we get our rackets and Pam passes out tennis balls. They smell lovely. I roll one over my hand, feel the felt coating. We try to bounce it on the strings, keep it in the air. I manage to do it three times without dropping it. Bang bang girl is brilliant at everything. Flori is hopeless which makes me feel *much* better.

Minxie sits by the net, trainer off, rubbing her foot.

"I'm *so* bored," she says. Pam ignores her.

Bang bang girl comes over and speaks very quietly to me.

"Try gripping the racket like this," she says.

She shows me and I say thanks.

"That's a great racket."

"Thanks."

"I'm Sarah."

"I'm Gemma," I say.

Pam gathers us together. "Right, forehands, great place to start. What do we all know?" Everyone knows a lot. Apart from me and Flori, of course. Even the twins can show Pam how to take the racket back to hit the ball.

Pam goes to one side of the net with a basket of balls. She tells us to get in a line. I go straight to the back, even manage to tuck myself behind Flori who is almost stuck to the netting.

Pam starts throwing balls for us. Minxie's shot looks good. Sarah blasts the ball, fast and wide. Pam calls out things I don't understand like, "Great point of contact, Minxie... Remember the loop, Sarah."

Bradley's shot goes in the net. Raj whacks it so hard it smashes into the back netting. He has a second shot and almost hits Pam. The first twin swings and misses and the second twin thinks it's his turn but Pam tells the first twin to try again and they end up fighting and Pam tells them to pick up balls. Flori stands with her feet locked to the back line. The ball comes and she taps it on the third bounce. It rolls into the net.

It's my turn. I think about my grip and my feet and hitting the ball. Pam throws it to me. I take the racket back like she showed us and miss it completely. Minxie bursts out laughing. I can feel her behind me, spinning round and covering her mouth.

"None of that, Minx," says Pam, pointing her racket like a long, cross finger. "Try again, Gemma."

She throws the ball to me again. It soars over the net towards me. I move and take my racket back and I hit it. I hit the ball high over the net and down the side of the court. I watch as it sails through the air and lands in the court.

Pam looks at me and says, "Great shot, how did it feel, Gemma?"

And I say, "Good."

But it didn't feel good.

It felt fantastic.

Chapter Nineteen

At lunchtime, we fetch our packed lunches and find a place to eat. Minxie is on her own in the clubhouse. I feel bad leaving her there but she has her headphones on and I really don't want to be with her. I join Sarah and Flori on the benches outside, under the covered deck.

Joe has packed me two filled rolls, crisps, fruit and a chocolate bar. I stare at it, wondering how much I can eat.

"That's one huge lunch!" says Sarah. "Your mum's given you enough for the week!"

I smile. "It wasn't my mum."

"Oh," says Sarah.

"My mum's on a cruise in the Caribbean." It feels really grown-up saying that, as if we are always jetting off to hot places. I bite into a roll.

"Wow," says Flori. "Are you, like, really rich?"

I can't help it, but I laugh out loud at that, spurt bread and ham into my lap. "No!" I say. "Her friend Jerry won it in a competition. He looks after rescued animals."

"Oh," says Flori. "I won a bike in a competition once. But I never rode it." Sarah laughs and I laugh too and it feels good. "I gave it away in the end," says Flori. "To the boy over the road."

We are quiet for a bit, each of us eating. Sarah throws crumbs to a little bird pecking near our feet.

"That book you're reading, Flori," I say. "I read it last term. It's good."

She looks at me and smiles a little, pushes her headband back up. "I like the way Amy and Jay become friends."

"Yeah." I nod. "It's great." I slip my trainers off and stretch my feet on the grass. They're rubbing a little. I glance at the others. "Did you want to play tennis this week?" I ask.

"Of course," says Sarah.

"Absolutely, incredibly, honestly, NO!" says Flori. "But Mum booked it. She and Pam are friends. I've done her a deal. I'll do the two weeks if I *don't* have to go to swim camp."

"Oh!" I say. "I would *love* to go to swim camp."

Flori makes a vomit sound which makes me smile.

"How long has your mum gone away for?" asks Sarah.

"A month."

"Wow," she says. "So was that your dad who dropped you off this morning in that cool car?"

"No, that was Joe, my uncle. He made the massive lunch!"

"Oh."

"Could you not stay with your dad?" asks Flori.

There it is again. The question about my dad. I fold my crisp packet and take out the tangerine. I'm not sure what to say so I just say, "No."

"Oh," says Flori.

Sarah offers her chocolates round. Raj runs over and takes one. Then the twins see there is chocolate on offer and they come over and argue about who should have the square ones. Sarah goes into the kitchen to find a bowl to tip them into and the boys all follow her, Flori skipping behind saying the square ones are her favourite too. I stare out at the court, start to peel my tangerine. It feels like Flori's question about my dad still hangs in the air, unanswered.

It's just known at home that I don't have a dad.

But in the last two days I've been asked about him twice. And I know nothing. I have nothing to say. For the first time in my life it feels strange. I wonder if Joe knows anything about him.

I have *so much* finding out to do.

There is a shriek from the clubhouse. Minxie stomps out, headphones still on. I smile a little. I think the chocolate crew flushed her out.

Chapter Twenty

Sophie meets us at two. She bounds over and hugs Bradley and then wraps her arm around me. "How did it go, Gemma?" she asks. "You all look exhausted!" I nod and say fine and we climb into her car. She tells me to get in the front. "Bradley's not quite tall enough yet." He grunts and picks up his hand-held game console.

Sophie hands us drink cartons and cookies. "I've just got to check with Pam about a wet weather plan." She dashes into the clubhouse and I watch them chatting.

"Does your mum play?" I ask Bradley.

"Yep," he says, pressing buttons. "She helps here with the juniors sometimes. She's good. But not as good as Joe – he's *awesome*!"

Bradley knows more about Joe than I do. Everyone does.

Sophie runs back to the car and we drive away. The radio comes on and Bradley starts moaning about having to miss a sleepover and that his game console isn't fully charged and I'm pleased I don't have to talk.

We go over the river and soon we are on the long road with the tunnel of trees. We rumble over the level crossing and turn down a country lane into a different village. The car stops at a white cottage. There is a wooden door with a metal knocker and a black and white cat sitting on the step.

"Do you mind just grabbing a bag of shopping?" says Sophie, and we climb out and get bags from the boot.

The cat stands up as we walk past and stretches his front legs.

"That's Bobby," says Sophie. "He loves a cuddle."

I put the bag down and tickle him under the chin. He wraps himself round my legs, twisting in and out, purring so loudly that I can feel the rumble in his tummy.

I stroke him over and over and then walk into the kitchen and help Sophie unpack. The kitchen is cosy. There is a string of checked bunting over the shelves and big wooden beams on the ceiling. On the windowsill are framed photos. Sophie, Bradley and his dad. They make such a lovely family. Bradley and his dad stand with tennis rackets, Bradley beaming at the camera, his dad smiling and proud.

"What's your favourite thing to eat?" says Sophie, pulling out packets of pork pie and crisps.

I look at her and say, "All of this!" and she laughs.

"You must tell me what you *don't* like, Gemma."

"Um ... pineapple, prawns and, oh, that chickpea hummus dip. Mum's friend Jerry makes it in huge batches and I *hate* it!"

Sophie lifts a tub out of the bag and says, "You are banned, hummus! Back of the fridge for you!" and we both smile.

"Joe gave me a *massive* lunch today!"

Sophie laughs and puts the frozen things away. "It's always amazed me how much that man eats! He must have had his own tummy in mind!"

"Have you known Joe long?"

She shuts the freezer and looks round at me. "Ooh, yes, many years." She smiles again but it's an odd smile this time, a bit sad. "He was best friends with Bradley's dad." She unwraps the bananas, ripping the plastic wrapper. And then she starts to speak again but her mobile phone rings and she picks it up to see who it is.

"Work call," she says, glancing at the screen. "I better take it. Sorry, Gemma, I'll be quick," and she disappears out of the kitchen.

I put the apples in the fruit bowl. I wonder what happened with Joe and Bradley's dad. She said they *were* best friends. Did they fall out at the same time as Joe and Mum and Gran? I wonder if it's all mixed up together.

I look round at the other photos. The fridge is covered in them. Sophie comes back in. "Sorry about that, Gemma. This new client is super fussy!"

Bradley wanders in, clicking two pieces of Lego together. "They are *all* fussy," he says.

"No, they're not!" laughs Sophie.

"What sort of clients do you have?" I ask.

"I'm a designer. Interiors. I make places look nice, I suppose."

"Or revolting," says Bradley, making a vomit sound. "That one with the purple stuff was yuck."

"Yes, that was a bit out there!" says Sophie. "Come and see the cat foster area and meet Mungo."

"You foster *cats*?"

"Yes," says Sophie. "Bobby is ours. But we always

have a rescue. One that needs help while we try to find their real home or a new home. Mungo was very thin and poorly when he came but he's getting better now."

Bradley grabs a banana and follows us. "Mungo's staying," he says. "He's not going anywhere."

"Brads," says Sophie, quite sharply. "We're trying to find his real owner. You know that." Bradley ignores her, peels his banana and takes a bite.

"Do they get on?" I ask. "Bobby and Mungo?"

"They don't mix," says Sophie. "We foster cats on a short-term basis so we have to keep them separate and not let them outside."

"They'll mix when Mungo stays," says Bradley, shoving the rest of the banana into his mouth. "Come and see." He waves me to follow him.

The cat area is at the back of the house in the conservatory. I can't see Mungo at first but Bradley finds him straight away. He is curled in the corner in the sunshine. We kneel down next to him and Bradley strokes his head. Mungo is beautiful. He has a furry M shape on his forehead and black stripes all over his body. Mungo peels himself up and Bradley lifts him and tucks him into his body.

"He was macy ... macky..." Bradley turns to Sophie. "What's that word again?"

"Emaciated," says Sophie, quietly. "We think he had travelled quite a long way from home and got stuck in an allotment shed. He was horrendously thin when he came to us and his beautiful tabby fur was very scraggy, but he's on the mend now."

Bradley strokes the top of his head.

"It's been a long journey," says Sophie. "And he wasn't microchipped, so finding the owner is proving tricky."

"It must be hard to let the cats go," I say, reaching out to tickle his ears.

"Yes, sometimes. But we have to. That's our job. We've fostered many, many cats."

"No one wants him," says Bradley. "Or they would have found him. You've had him on Facebook for ages now and put up posters in all the vets' surgeries."

"Don't start, Brad," says Sophie, raising her eyebrows at him.

"Did you help Joe with Carrot Cake?" I ask.

"Yes, I had to convince Joe to take him on. And whatever that man says, he absolutely *adores* him!"

I smile. "He calls him a waste of space."

"It's all a show, Gemma," says Sophie, laughing. "You should have seen him when Carrot took his first proper steps again. Great big tears pouring down his face!"

I laugh and Bradley gently puts Mungo down. "Like I'll be," says Bradley. "If Mungo goes." He runs out of the conservatory and I hear him thudding up the stairs and the sharp slam of a door.

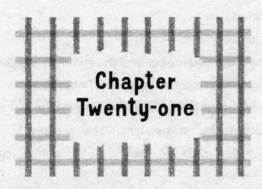

Chapter
Twenty-one

"Fancy fish and chips?" says Joe as we drive home from Sophie's.

"Yes, please," I say. I loosen my laces, let my feet stretch a bit.

"Did you enjoy it, Gem, the tennis?" he asks. "Be honest."

"Yeah, it was good but super hard too. There's *so* much to learn."

"Well, Pam was very impressed."

"Oh, how do you know that?"

"She told Sophie that you had natural talent."

It makes it sounds like I've been doing a test or something.

"How was Minxie?" asks Joe.

I want to say that I don't like her. I really don't like her.

But instead I say, "She's a good player."

"Mmmm."

"Can I ask you something?"

"Anything," says Joe but he shifts in his seat and glances at me as if he's worried about what I want to know.

"It was a bit odd when Pam first met me." I stop, try to get the words right. "She seemed kind of fascinated to meet me, like she'd been waiting for me or something."

Joe taps the steering wheel. He's quiet.

"Are you really famous or something?" I say, smiling at him. "I've been told you're really good at tennis! Do they all think you've taught me?"

He tips his head back and laughs. "Oh, I'd be a terrible teacher!"

"You wouldn't!"

We rattle across the level crossing. I look both ways, down the long straight railway tracks and think how odd it is that we can drive on them. A minute or two later and we reach the tunnel of trees. The sunlight filters through, dappling the road.

Joe didn't answer my questions. It feels a bit odd. I'm tired and my foot aches and I think about my home and my friends and I feel a little homesick.

"Could I speak to Mum later?" I ask. "Sorry, I can't phone abroad on my mobile."

"Of course!" says Joe. He presses a few buttons on the dashboard and a ringing sound echoes through the car. He did it super fast, as if he realized the phone call would stop me asking him any other tricky things.

"Oh, I meant later..." I say, but Mum's voice is suddenly in the car, all around me.

"Hello," she says.

Joe doesn't say anything. I think he's seeing this as my call so I say, "Hi, Mum. It's me."

"Oh, Gem, love, how wonderful."

"I can't believe we're talking to you on the ship! How is it?"

"Hot. Great. The food's amazing." She tells us about the delicious giant prawns and how Jerry squealed really loudly as the heads were pulled off and the waiter thought he was ill. Jerry would *never* eat an animal.

"What have you been doing?" she says. "I miss you, Gem."

"I've been at tennis camp today."

Joe puts his sunglasses on and fiddles with the air-con dials.

Mum is quiet, just the crackle of the phone line, all

the way from some giant ship. I wonder if we've been cut off.

"Are you there, Mum?"

"Yes, I'm here," she says. I thought she'd be thrilled. She's always wanting me to try new things, not just swim all the time.

I wonder if she's cross I wasn't with Joe.

"Joe had to work today," I explain.

"Oh," she says.

Quiet again.

And then she says, "Can you put Joe on the phone, please, Gem?"

"He's right here!" I shriek, excited I can say that. "You're on speakerphone! He's just picked me up and we're going for fish and chips."

"Joe," says Mum. "Did I hear that right? About the camp?"

Joe shifts in his seat, grips the steering wheel again, stops at the traffic lights.

"Carrie, I had to sort something..."

I don't want him having to explain so I cut in.

"I really liked it, Mum! I'm going *all* this week and next."

"Are you?" she says, very slowly and quietly.

"Yes, and Joe bought me new sports gear, and a racket and trainers." I look at Joe, hoping he'll be nodding in agreement but he's wincing a little, his mouth pulled, eyes a bit scrunched.

No one speaks. It feels like everything I say is wrong right now. I'm not sure if I should say anything else.

"I'll need to pay you back for all that, Joe," says Mum. Her voice is completely different now, like it is when she's on the phone to the electricity company or the bank.

"There's no need," says Joe. "You know that."

And then I get it. Mum's annoyed that Joe has sent me to this fancy tennis camp and bought me new gear and stuff we could never afford.

"Maybe we can speak later, Joe?" she says.

"Yes," says Joe. "No problem. We're having a great time. I just needed to get Gemma some kit to wear, that's all."

Joe said that to try to make things better. But it won't help *at all*.

There are voices in the background. I hear Jerry shout that they're going to the pool and Mum should join them.

"I'll see you there," she calls out. Jerry shouts back and we wait while they sort out their plans. I look out of the window, watch the fields flash by.

Everything is quiet again. Mum is waiting for us to speak. It feels a bit odd so I say, "Wow, the ship has a pool."

"Yes, only a small one," says Mum. "You can't do lengths, just bob around a bit." I hear her sigh a little.

"Well," I say, "that's good, Mum. Bobbing's your best stroke."

"Cheeky," she says.

I know she's smiling. It's funny that. She's on the other side of the world in a big ship on the ocean and I can't see her but I can tell by how she says those words that she is smiling.

We pull into Joe's road.

"We're home," he says. "Enjoy the pool, Carrie."

"I'll speak to you very soon, Gem," says Mum. "I love you."

"OK," I say. I'm desperate to make things all sunshiney again, so I say, "And Mum, you were so right about Joe!"

"Was I?" says Mum.

"Yep, everyone loves him!"

I can hear her take a breath, a sort of gaspy, short breath and then she says, "Yes, Gem, everyone does. Speak soon, love," and she is gone.

Joe parks the car and switches off the engine. He leans back in his seat and sighs a little. I feel bad for him.

He's tried so hard to make things good for me. I wonder if I should say something about Mum and how she can get all funny about money and stuff but I don't think I need to. I think Joe knows.

"Quick shower," says Joe. "And we'll get fish and chips."

I nod and open my door.

"Thanks," I say. I want to ask if we are seeing Lexi and Minxie but I don't.

And then Joe says, "Just us tonight, Gem," and it's like he knew exactly what I was thinking.

"Great," I say, and I worry that I sound a little too pleased we aren't seeing them.

Chapter Twenty-two

The fish and chips are the best ever. Mum and I normally get one large fish and share it and it's never quite enough. Joe orders me a medium all of my own, with chips and salt and vinegar. The batter is really crunchy. Joe has mushy peas and we laugh when I say he'd have to pay me a million pounds to eat them.

We talk about forehands and spin and looping the ball and all the shots. Joe knows everything. And I know so little.

"Minxie was wrong about Pam," I say. "I like her."

Joe smiles. "Minxie is wrong about a *lot* of things. Don't be too hard on her. She's had a rough time the last few years."

"Does that mean she's allowed to be unkind and rude?" I say, shoving a large piece of cod in my mouth, the batter crunching around it. So yum.

Joe looks at me, smiles a little as if my comment surprised him and shakes his head. "No, no, it doesn't." He loads up his fork, the peas topping each layer. "I don't think she really wants to be there. Her dad, Geoff, is chairman of the club. She's a nice player but he is desperate for her to be brilliant. She's had loads of coaching."

"Mmm," I say, reaching for the ketchup. "That's a bit like Surinder's mum with netball. Her mum makes her go to *all* the sessions. She had to miss a party last week for a match. They had the biggest row."

Joe puts his cutlery down. "That's tough," he says. "I hope her mum listens to what she has to say."

"Sometimes," I say, "but not always."

He scoops up more peas and I make a yuck sound.

"Did you have lots of coaching?" I ask.

He takes a swig of his beer and peers at me over the bottle. "A bit, but many years ago."

"I saw the photo of you in the clubhouse, with the trophy."

"Yes, that was a good day. Next stop Wimbledon!"

He turns to stack the dishwasher and his phone rings. He looks at the screen. "I just need to take this," he says and I'm not sure if it's my mum, still cross about all the new expensive things, or Lexi, still cross that I'm taking up Joe's time.

I'm a bit of a problem right now for Joe.

I reach over to get my phone from the side and message the girls. Carrot Cake jumps on to my lap.

Gemma: I survived the first day!

Jess: fab! well done 🛡️

Gemma: Joe's friend picked me up – she fosters cats – rescue ones

Jess: cute.

Surinder: OMG I'd be sneezing all day long

Jess: the puppy barks at cats. he chased one across the garden.

Surinder: I saw Nicola today.
she completely ignored me!!!!!
she was with a girl we don't know.

Jess: Her cousins staying

Surinder: Oh

Gemma: She might not have seen u

Surinder: She saw me

Gemma: Carrot Cake is on my lap purring.
He's adorable.

Surinder: I go away tomorrow. Camping for a
whole week in Devon. 😩 wish me luck.

Jess: Sounds lovely

Gemma: Mum and I went to Devon.
It's beautiful.

Surinder: ⛺ 🥱

Jess: 😆

Gemma: 🍀 🤞 💕 💎 🌈 ✉️ ✳️ 👍 💞

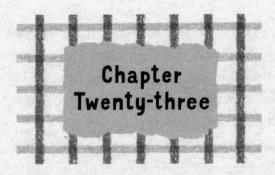

Chapter
Twenty-three

I wake to the sound of rain. The patter on the roof is like something from a movie. At home, I can hear the rain bouncing off the roofs of the buses that rattle past my window. But not above me, like now. The only thing I hear above me at home is Mrs Dawkins' walking frame tapping across the floor and her TV, of course.

Joe knocks on the door. "You awake, Gem?" he says.

"Yep."

"We need to leave a bit earlier to help dry the courts."

"OK." I stare at my skort and tracksuit and the fresh socks I laid out last night. Part of me wants to just curl up with my book in my leggings and sparkly T-shirt. But part of me is ready to give it a go again, try to hit the ball over the net and in between the lines.

We pull up at the club and Pam is there, sweeping the courts, brushing the water to the side. Joe gets out and helps her, the water sprinkling over the bottom of his smart trousers. I take a broom and join in too. It's stopped raining and I'm glad.

Minxie's car pulls up. She gets out and heads for the clubhouse.

The twins arrive wearing the same tops.

"Blimey, it's hard enough already," says Pam. "How can I tell you apart today?"

Flori dashes on to court and hurries to the back corner, her face hidden in the pages of her book. She has a different hairband on today, a wide red velvet one with yellow stars. Her mum beeps the car horn loudly as she leaves, yelling out of the window, "Love you, darling. Join in, won't you!"

Sarah arrives and the two of us wander over to Flori.

"Can't I just stay here," she says, "stuck to the carpet?"

"No!" we both shout, laughing as we pull her up. When everyone is there, we start.

"Lots to learn today," says Pam. "We're going to have two coaches and split you into two groups. Those who've played quite a bit and those who are wonderfully new to the game."

"Oh, you're joking!" says Minxie. "A new coach! Nightmare. I think I'd rather stay with you, Pam." She bounces a ball hard on the ground and it flies high into the air.

"Well, it's your lucky day, Minxie. You are with me. And so are Raj, Bradley and Sarah. The rest of you are with my son Jake."

"Jake!" says Minxie. She stares at Pam, her eyes wide and blinking. The ball she was bouncing rolls away and lands in a puddle by the netting. "Jake's coming ... here."

Pam smiles a little. "Yes, in about ten minutes. Now go and get that ball, Minx, before it's soaking wet."

We warm up and go over what we learned yesterday and then Pam talks about the backhand. You have to hold the racket differently. Two hands on the grip. You have to think about your balance and your feet and your body shifting weight and it's almost impossible. Flori sends her ball sky-high. Max hits the net. Finlay hits Pam, right bang in her tummy. Sarah smashes her shot across the court and Minxie glides hers beautifully over the net. Then she smiles and says, "Ooh, was that in? I'm not sure!"

She giggles and tucks her hair behind her ears and

pulls her skirt straight and skips round to Pam's side with four balls to go in the ball feeder. It's like a new Minxie has arrived. And then I realize why. The gate bangs and Jake walks in. He is tall and smiley and has the coolest hair.

Bradley is about to hit.

"Great ready position!" shouts Jake. He watches Bradley hit the ball. "Wow! Cool shot!" Bradley beams and races round to pick up his balls.

Raj gets ready.

Sarah tucks behind me in line.

"Jake's county champion," she says, leaning into me as if I need information quickly. "Last two years, under-eighteens champ. He is amazing. Epic talent." And then she jigs up and down, pulls on her racket strings as if they need lining up again, whips her racket through the air to get the swing right.

Minxie runs behind us and gets in line. Her eyes are firmly planted on Jake, one hand twisting at a curl she has pulled free from her ponytail.

We split into groups. I feel a bit sorry for Jake being with us. I've never played, Flori looks like she'd rather be in prison and the twins trip over themselves and their rackets.

"Right, you two," he says. He digs around in Pam's big red sports bag and pulls out two T-shirts. "I made these last night." He passes one twin a white T-shirt with *MAX* written on it and the other one a T-shirt with *FINLAY* on it. The names are written in big red marker-pen letters.

"Wicked," says Max, putting his on.

"We're here to play tennis," says Jake. "No fighting, no squabbling, just tennis. Got it?" They look up at him and nod like he's an Egyptian god.

"Minxie!" yells Pam. "It's your turn, on *this* court." I watch Minxie as she peels her eyes away from Jake and slumps back to Pam.

We practise backhands and then we put the two shots together. Forehand, backhand. We throw balls for each other. I go with Flori. She tries but most of the time she misses the ball completely. Jake shows her again. She takes a giant swing but she misses the ball and whacks her knee. She slumps to the ground and her headband falls off. I race over and pick it up. One of the yellow stars has come off.

"I'm so sorry, Flori," I say, passing it to her. She squints up at me, rubbing her knee, trying not to cry.

"It's OK," she says, sliding the headband back in place. "Thanks for helping." I pick up the yellow star and put it in my pocket to give her later. I'm worried she'll be upset if she sees it has fallen off.

The twins start arguing about throwing the ball properly, so Jake splits them up and I hit with Max. We work well together. We even manage to hit a rally, ten shots in a row.

Jake counts the shots, one to ten and then claps madly and shouts, "Fantastic job!" and when I look over at Minxie she makes a face at me as if I'm showing off or something.

Chapter Twenty-four

We eat lunch on the bench outside again. I have a chicken wrap today and a vanilla yoghurt. So yum.

Max and Finlay come over and ask for chocolate.

"Not today," says Sarah and they wander off.

I rustle in my pocket and find the yellow star. "This came off your headband, Flori." I pass it to her. "Sorry."

She takes it and slips it in her bag. "I'm so glad," she says. "I've tried to get them off but Mum used superglue."

Sarah lets out a giggle and secretly passes us a bag of chocolates and we share them before the twins can see.

After lunch, we sit with Jake and watch the other four play a game.

"They all know how to score," he says. "I'm going to talk you through it and then we'll have a go. OK?"

They start a proper game with scores and serves.

Bradley and Sarah playing Raj and Minxie. Pam helps them to stand in the right position and gives them tips.

Minxie is a different person. She runs and chases and shouts "good shot" to Raj. When Pam tells her to stand closer to the net to volley she says, "Oh, of course."

She does a really good return and when Jake says, "Good shot, Minxie," she looks over and beams a huge smile and bounces back to wait for the next point. It's like someone's flicked a switch in her.

Scoring is so confusing. The points aren't one or two but fifteen and thirty and forty and something called deuce and advantage. And some players switch places and some don't. Some move back, some stay still.

"You have to defend and attack," says Jake.

"It's like chess," says Max. "I'm good at chess."

"No, you're not," says Finlay. But Jake has seated them well apart and Max doesn't hear.

"It *is* a bit like chess," laughs Jake. "You have to position yourself carefully and decide when it's the right time to move. Tennis is just a little more active."

He turns back to the players. "Right, what's the score now?" he asks..

"Love—thirty," says Flori.

"Excellent," says Jake. "You've picked that up super

130

fast." Flori pushes her headband back on her head and smiles and it suits her.

We play our own game after that. Jake is super helpful but it is a complete muddle. Flori and I get the giggles as we keep bumping into each other.

Chapter Twenty-five

Sophie picks me and Bradley up and takes us out for ice cream. The café has huge dairy cows painted on the pink walls. There are more flavours of ice cream than I have ever seen.

"Try something new," says Sophie.

I ask to try mango tango sorbet and the girl behind the counter puts some on a tiny spoon for me. I order one scoop of that and one of double chocolate with sprinkles. We sit on high stools, looking out over a courtyard with big plants and gravel.

"How was it today?" asks Sophie, dipping her spoon into her tutti frutti.

"Amazing!" says Bradley, biting the flake on his raspberry ripple. "Jake was there. He is SO awesome."

"Yes, he certainly is!" laughs Sophie.

"I felt bad," I say and then I stop because I'm not sure it sounds right.

"Why?" asks Sophie.

"Um, well." I lick my spoon, dig it back into the sorbet. "He had my group and we can't do much!"

"We all start somewhere," says Sophie. "Minxie and Bradley have been playing since they were five."

"Why didn't you?" says Bradley, his eyes slanted at me, his mouth gripped on the little wooden spoon. He has chocolate all round his mouth. I can feel Sophie watch me too, as if she wants to hear what I might say.

I shake my head, shrug. "I just didn't."

"I know there was a two-day agreement between you and Joe," says Sophie and I smile at her. "So today was day two. Can you manage day three?"

I nod, swing my legs, tap my trainers against the wooden bench. I loved it today. I want to keep playing, keep learning.

"Think so," I say and Sophie leans into me and says, "Good stuff," and we get up and put our ice-cream tubs in the bin.

Back at Sophie's, Bradley checks on Mungo and then dives on his Lego, the sound of him raking through the boxes rattling through the house.

"Sounds like he's struggling to find the right pieces," says Sophie.

"I can help," I say.

"You sure?"

"I can try!" It feels good to do something helpful.

I find Bradley. He is scooping his hands through one of the giant boxes.

"Which bits do you need?" I ask. He shows me a small grey brick with two circles on it. It's like a tiny pair of binoculars.

"It connects," he says.

I nod and start rummaging.

"Are you following a kit?" I ask.

"Making my own," he says, not looking up. "I've designed it. It's a massive spaceship, large enough for a troop of stargazers."

"Cool," I say. I find one of the vital pieces. "Bingo!" I pass it to him.

"Wicked," he says. "I just need four more now."

"Is your dad good at Lego?" I ask, tipping out another box to sort.

Bradley stops sorting. He puts both hands on the box and looks up at me. He bites his bottom lip and he says, "My dad died."

I stare at him, my mouth a little open. "I'm so sorry. I didn't know."

He looks down again, scoops more bricks. "It's OK."

"How long ago?" I wonder if that's a stupid question to ask.

He tilts his head and squeezes his face as if he's thinking. "I was six. I'm eight now." And then he turns back to sorting and spreading and I do too and soon we've found the four vital pieces. "Wicked," says Bradley and he lays them out, ready for construction. "Could you find four of these?" He holds up a red square brick, four by two.

"I'll try," I say and I run my hands through the bricks. We sit for a bit, both busy with our tasks. It doesn't take long to find them.

Bradley picks up his model and says, "Is your dad alive?"

I stop for a second, sit back on my heels, one hand filtering through the Lego.

"I don't know," I say.

He stares at me. "Why?" he asks.

"I don't know anything about my dad," I say and he nods a little as if that makes sense and turns back to linking pieces.

I pass him the red bricks.

"Thanks," he says. "You're good at this."

I get to my feet. "I'm going to get a drink," I say. "Want one?"

He shakes his head. He doesn't look up but he is talking to himself a little, planning out his new mega ship, deep in construction mode.

I feel so bad for asking him about his dad. And then I couldn't answer something so simple about my own dad. It makes me feel a bit tearful. I go out to the garden and find Sophie weeding the veggie patch. She sees me and smiles and passes me a fresh strawberry.

"Try it, straight from the patch."

I bite it. It's delicious.

"I hope I haven't upset Bradley," I say.

"Oh, Gemma, I'm sure it's fine. What happened?" She turns back to the weeds.

"I didn't know about his dad. I'm sorry."

Sophie stands up and takes off her gloves. "Oh gosh, Gemma, it's my fault, I thought you knew."

I shake my head. "I feel so bad for asking about him."

"Don't worry!" she says, smiling. "We talk about him all the time. Brad won't mind. I thought Joe had told you but I suppose it has all been a whirlwind since you arrived." She gives me a quick hug, makes me feel better. "He died two years ago. He was very ill. Joe and Chris were great friends. Like brothers, really. Joe is Bradley's godfather. It's been a tough time and he's been an absolute rock to me and Brad."

Joe and Chris were best friends.

That makes sense now.

I think of the photo of them all. How could someone so young die?

Bobby wanders up to Sophie and she scoops him up, buries herself in his fur.

"Let's have a cup of tea," she says and I nod and follow her inside. Sophie flicks the kettle on and then Bradley screeches to come and see and we dash into Mungo's room and Bradley is bent over, his back flat like a tabletop and Mungo is sitting on his back, staring at us.

Chapter
Twenty-six

Sophie drives me home. Bradley has brought his game console and earphones and he is madly pressing buttons and grunting at the screen. We get to the level crossing. The red lights start flashing and the alarm sounds. Sophie stops and puts on the brake and after a few seconds a pair of huge gates come down in front of the car.

A faint drizzle starts. Sophie turns off the engine. Bradley hisses, "Get out of it."

I glance round. He is head down, engrossed in the game.

We sit and wait. The rain falls harder now, running down the windscreen in great, wiggling lines.

"I don't know my dad," I say. Sophie turns her head to me and shifts a little in her seat so she can look at me more easily. "I've never met him."

Sophie nods. I think she knows. I can tell she's not sure what to say.

The train arrives. It thunders past. The car seems to shake a little. The carriages fly by, flicking past us like those little paper movies you make when you draw a picture in the corner of every page and then flick it really fast. And then it's gone and everything is quiet. Sophie starts up the car and puts on the wipers.

"Your mum sounds incredible," she says.

I watch the wipers, sink a little in my seat.

"She is," I say. "We've never talked about my dad."

Sophie is quiet for a moment and then she says, "There is always time for these things."

"I've never asked about him," I say.

I'm hoping Sophie might know a few things, fill in the gaps, but it feels odd talking about it. I've never talked to *anyone* about my dad. Not even Mum. It just never seemed to matter. But now people are asking, and I've got no answers.

The gates lift. Sophie drives the car over the tracks. I look to my left and all I can see, for a very long way, are the railway lines going on and on.

"I'm sure you and your mum will make the right decisions when you need to," says Sophie.

I nod. Mum and I do make decisions together. But normally it's about Friday takeout and what TV show to watch and which swim galas I should go to. Not about my dad and if I should meet him.

"One more level!" yells Bradley, as if he's forgotten he has his headphones on. Sophie gives him the thumbs up.

I search for the little chapel with the lit candles at Christmas. I don't know if it's here or not. The fields all look the same. We turn on to the long road and then drive through the tunnel of leaves.

"I love this bit," I say.

"It *is* lovely," says Sophie. "In the winter it's just plain sky and the trees are all spindly and now we get this wonderful festival of green." I lean forward and angle my head to see better but then Sophie says, "This is fun sometimes," and she presses a button and a cover pulls back in the roof and there's a window there and I can sit back in the seat and look up at the leaves above us. "Gosh," she says, "We haven't done this since Chris was alive. We used to do it every summer."

I watch the leaves, watch as the rain falls on the glass and then we are out of the leafy tunnel and it's just grey clouds.

"I'm glad Bradley has all the photos," I say, trying to

work out the best way to say it. "All the photos of him and his dad."

"Yes," says Sophie. "The memories are very important to us."

And then Bradley bangs the seat so hard it makes us both jump a little. He peels off the headphones, throws them down and yells, "Got him! Wicked!"

Sophie smiles and says, "Thank goodness. It can go either way with that game. The monsters win and it's not a happy time!"

We drive on in silence for a bit. I think about Chris and Joe.

"Were you at Joe's wedding, all those years ago?" I ask.

Sophie smiles and says, "Yes, I was, with Chris. He was Joe's best man. You were a super-cute bridesmaid!"

"Do you know my mum?"

"Not well," says Sophie. "I didn't meet her until the wedding."

We arrive at Joe's house. She parks up.

"So you only knew her after she'd fallen out with Gran and Joe?"

She nods and sits back in her seat. "Joe is just so, so happy to be spending this time with you," she says.

"It's a bit hard ... not knowing what went on. I'm trying

to find out more. I want to make things better."

Sophie twists to look at me. "Oh, Gem..." she starts. "That's so tricky..."

Joe opens the front door, his mobile pinned to his ear, talking rapidly. He makes a sorry sign as if to say he won't be able to get away.

"Do you know what happened, Sophie?" I ask.

She stares ahead, watches Joe go back into the house. "I know a bit, Gem, but I'm really not the right person to tell you stuff. That has to be Joe and your mum."

"Mum doesn't know I'm trying to find out."

"Oh," says Sophie. She tilts her head, pats me on the shoulder. "Maybe you should ask her about it."

I laugh a little. "Mmm ... that won't work."

"It might now," says Sophie. "Now that you're here."

We sit for a moment and then I say, "No one wants to tell me anything." I can feel a tear brewing so I open my door. "Thanks for the lift," I say and I climb out.

"See you tomorrow, Gem," she says. "Talk to Joe." She shouts the last bit out as if she feels bad for not helping me.

I wave at her and walk towards the open door. I'm irritated now, not ready to go in, so while Sophie backs up and pulls away, I pretend to look for something in my bag and when she is gone, I sit on the front step. It's damp from the rain but I don't care. Carrot runs over and climbs on my lap.

"No one will tell me anything, Carrot," I say, stroking his soft fur. "And the strangest thing is that I think it's because it's all linked to me." I pull him close, his tummy rumbling. "Everything that went on, I think it's linked to *me* and that's why they *can't* say anything, even if they wanted to."

I've had a feeling a *bit* like this before, not long ago. Nicola didn't invite me to her party. I knew Jess and Surinder were hiding something from me. Jess hates stuff like that. She looked nervous all week. All the hidden whispers and broken chats when I appeared. And then on Friday, walking out of school, Surinder had called out, "See you tomorrow, Gem," and the other girls had whipped round and Surinder had slapped her hand over her mouth and I knew right then what was going on.

There was a big fuss. *I could only invite three ... the car only takes four*, that kind of thing. Nicola's mum had even called that night to see if I *could* come but my mum was super nice and said we had plans. We didn't have plans. We hardly ever do. But Mum called in sick the next day and took me to a theme park with rides that turn you upside down. She even bought me burger and chips. It was all *very* not my mum.

This feels like it felt that week.

Something is going on that everyone else knows about.

And it's about me.

I peel myself up from the front step. Carrot jumps off my lap and follows me inside. Joe is coming towards me, still talking. He tilts the phone and just says, "Day two go OK?"

I nod and say, "Great," because the tennis was great, better than great. I head upstairs for a shower, my mind buzzing with all the finding-out I have to do.

Chapter Twenty-seven

There are so many new words to learn. Baseline, tramline, service line. Stance, follow through, split step. We do forehands, backhands and the volley, when you hit it before it bounces. Sarah has an amazing volley and Pam uses her a lot to demonstrate.

"Not too close to the net," she yells as we all have a go. "Take a step back, Max!"

My trainers are starting to rub in a new place. And my hand is sore where I've gripped the racket. But the more we play, the easier some things get.

"You're really connecting with the ball now, Gemma," says Pam and I smile. "Third day of tennis. Impressive."

I want to ask so many things. How the racket should swing through, how exactly to do the "split step" but it's hard. If I ask, we stop playing and then Minxie gets all pouty and Bradley looks fed up and the twins mess around. I try to remember stuff to ask Joe.

"You mustn't stand in no man's land," says Pam as we play a game.

"Sorry," I say. "I'm not sure where no man's land is."

Minxie sniggers again.

"No man's land," says Pam, "is the space in between the two back lines. If you're there, the ball will land right at your feet. Make sure you are either back on the baseline or moving up the court. Don't worry! You'll soon get it, Gemma."

"I'm so glad you ask stuff," says Flori. "I haven't a clue." She tries to hit a backhand return but her shot goes way up high and lands over the netting. Minxie laughs, very loud.

I stare at her. I stare at her hard.

Sarah mutters, "Just ignore her."

Jake arrives. He dumps his bike and joins us on the court. Minxie shakes her hair and moves forward to serve and tells Finlay to move over at the net or she might just hit him. He moves the wrong way and she does hit him, right on his leg. She runs over, all concerned, and says sorry loads of times.

"Unbelievable," says Sarah.

"Is she for real?" says Flori, pushing her headband back up. It's plain gold today.

"Yep," I say.

"I'm fine!" says Finlay, waving her away, and they reset and Minxie goes back to serve.

"Minxie," calls Jake from the net.

"Yes," she says, pulling on her skirt.

"You need to throw that ball a little more in front of you when you serve. It's going behind your head."

"Oh, OK," she says, and then she giggles because she throws it *too* far in front this time and she has to let it drop. She stops and looks over at Jake but he has turned away and is talking to his mum.

Jake takes us one at a time on to the other court and feeds us balls. Lots of balls. He has a basket full of them. Forehands and backhands and volleys. Raj first, then Sarah. Then the twins. Then me. We go through the basics, shot by shot, and I ask lots of questions. I try to think of it all as I hit the ball.

"Back to the baseline, each time," says Jake. "Or you'll get caught in no man's land."

I nod.

"Sure you know where that is?" he says.

I point to the middle of the court, in between the

back and the middle. "Here," I say. "I'll get caught here."

"Excellent, Gemma."

I glance over at Minxie. She is watching us, waiting on the bench for her turn, chewing on her nails.

―――――――――――――――

Sophie picks us up. We get back to the house and I feel part of it. I know that Bobby will curl round your legs and if you pick him up, he nestles into you, under your chin. I know where the glasses are kept and how the toilet has to be flushed twice to work. I know that Bradley often watches TV in the big red chair, upside down, his feet over the side. I like the way Sophie is with the TV. She doesn't stress about it like Mum.

I help Sophie to feed the cats and we refill the large cat biscuit jar. She holds the bag high and I funnel them in and we laugh as they spill out over the sides, Bobby rustling round to eat the ones that escape.

Joe collects me quite late. We sit in the garden on deckchairs and Joe eats some dinner that Sophie saved for him.

Bradley taps on the window that looks out from the house. He's holding up Mungo, laughing and cuddling him.

We all smile but when Sophie turns back, her smile disappears and she closes her eyes and takes a deep breath.

"I had a call today," she says, looking at Joe. "Mungo's owner has been found. Elderly lady, been in hospital. Her daughter's friend saw one of my posters at the vet's. Mungo ran off while she was away and of course they had no idea he got trapped in an allotment shed. The old lady's back home now, pining for her cat. They're coming to collect him on Friday."

"Oh," says Joe. "That's not good news."

"Nope," says Sophie. "I'll have to tell him tonight. He'll be heartbroken."

"Do you want me to stay and tell him with you?"

She looks up at him, shakes her head. "No, it'll be fine. He knows the score. This is always the aim, the best outcome, to find the owner." But her words are slow and sad.

"Not this time, though," says Joe, very quietly.

"No," says Sophie. "Not this time."

Chapter Twenty-eight

It's hot today. We all collapse at lunchtime, slumped in the shade with our packed lunches.

Flori lies back, one hand over her eyes. "How many days left of this torture?"

"It's Friday tomorrow," says Sarah. "You've nearly done a whole week, Flori!"

"Another one to go, though..." says Flori with a sigh.

"You might start liking it," I say. "I thought I'd hate it but it's the *best*."

Flori makes a groaning sound. "It's just not my thing."

Bradley eats his lunch super fast and then he is back on court, whacking the ball against the practice wall. His eyes looked red this morning. I think Sophie must have told him about Mungo.

"My feet hurt," says Flori.

"Mine too," says Sarah.

"I've got a blister on my thumb." I show them the red peeling skin and the bubble of soreness.

Flori kneels up to look and pulls a face. "You see," she says. "Torture."

Minxie is a little bit away from us, lying on her tummy, drawing in a notebook, headphones on, her head moving gently to the music. She has magazines laid out in front of her. She looks calm and happy, as if she is doing what she loves. Every so often she picks up her sandwich and takes a bite.

My phone rings.

It's Joe. I jump up and walk over to the netting.

"How're you doing?" he says.

"I'm hot, and I have a blister, but fine."

"Ooh, sorry, Gem, I'll pick up some strong plasters. Do you mind if we go to the pub for dinner tonight?"

It feels really grown-up, my uncle asking me if I mind if we go out for dinner. Mum and I hardly ever eat out.

"Of course," I say. "Where?"

"At a pub nearby. Sophie's going to drop you home. I'll be back early."

"Great."

"It's with Lexi and Minxie. I promised I'd take them out."

"OK," I say, although I feel flat at that news. "See you later."

"Yep, thanks, Gem," he says and I press the end button. I glance at Minxie. She is sat up, sketching. I hope she brings that notebook tonight. She's nice when she's sketching.

Chapter
Twenty-nine

We drive to a village miles away. It's a gorgeous evening, the fields golden in the fading sunlight.

The pub is old with low beams and a big shaggy dog stretched out by the bar. Lexi and Minxie are already there, both bent over their phones.

"Hi," says Joe.

Lexi looks up and smiles but it's not a happy smile. It's like she's forcing her mouth to make that shape. "Nice of you to join us," she says, glancing at her watch.

"I'll get some drinks," says Joe. "Come and choose, Gem," and I follow him to the bar.

I look at all the bottles, lined up at the back, glowing and glistening with fancy labels.

"That fizzy orange is nice," he says, pointing to a row of glass bottles. I nod and he orders one.

We take the drinks over to the table. My drink is in a cute bubble bottle. I pour a bit in my glass. It sparkles and bounces off the giant ice cubes.

Joe sits next to Lexi. He leans round to speak to Minxie. "Can you put your phone away now, please?"

She sighs deeply and puts her phone on the bench.

Lexi shuffles closer to Joe, flicks her hair and puts her head on his shoulder. She's like an ice cube, super hard and frozen at first and then after a little while she warms up, her edges starting to melt. She and Joe start talking, their heads very close.

I sip my drink. It tastes so nice. Minxie examines her nails. A waitress leaves menus on the table. It's a bit awkward, the two of us sitting in silence.

"What were you drawing earlier?" I ask.

She shrugs. "Just stuff." She picks up a menu and stares at it.

"Oh," I say. I take a menu too, tap it on the edge of the table. "You hit the ball really well."

"You think?" she says, shifting in her seat and biting on one nail.

"Yeah, I do. I'd love to hit a forehand like you do."

She scoffs a bit at this and drinks her Coke. "It won't take you long," she says. "We all know *that*, of course."

I stare at her over my glass. "What do you mean?"

She glances at Joe and Lexi, like she's making sure they can't hear. "Well, it's in your blood, isn't it?"

She puts the menu upright, looks around the room.

"I've no idea what you're talking about," I say. "What's in my blood?"

Minxie looks at me and raises her eyebrows, pulls her mouth into a sort of "what … seriously?" expression. She flicks her hair over her shoulder, stirs her drink. I can tell she's deciding whether to say anything else. She shifts in her seat, taps her glass. "We've all been waiting for the great Gemma to hit the ball," she says. "See what she can do. It's all the club's been talking about, but of course no one's meant to *say* anything."

I drop my glass. It slips out of my hand and hits my leg, the expensive fizzy drink spilling down my jeans. The glass rolls away, under the bench. Minxie slides to one side to avoid the mess. Lexi and Joe are still talking deeply, heads together. I get up and hurry off, searching for the toilets. The pub is busy. I push past people, feeling small and tearful.

I catch the sign for the toilets and dive inside.

Luckily there is an empty cubicle. I lock the door and lean over slightly so that my hands are on my thighs, breathing hard. My jeans have a wet drink patch all down the right leg. I don't want a pee so I just flush the chain and try to stop the urge to cry, try to stop this feeling that is juddering through me. I was right. Everyone does know something about me.

I come out and wash my hands, rub my face, stare at myself in the mirror.

But of course no one's meant to say *anything...*

I think about Nicola's party again, the way it had all been hidden from me. The way Surinder had given it away.

Minxie has just done a Surinder. She's opened it up, a bit like the first thump of a piñata when the crêpe paper starts to break and a sweet falls out.

It's in your blood, isn't it...

What does she mean? It's all so odd. Minxie doesn't know me. Joe doesn't really. How can they all have been *talking* about me? I have so many questions and no one to answer them.

I dry my hands and pull open the door. Joe is outside, waiting for me.

"Are you OK, Gem? What happened?"

I shrug, shake my head.

"Did Minxie say something?"

I shrug again but this time I can't hold it in and I cry, quite hard, and he hugs me. We move to one side and he waits for the tears to stop.

"It's all just so confusing," I say. "Everyone seems to know stuff about me but no one will tell me anything."

Joe sighs and stares at me.

"OK," he says. "I'm sorry you're upset. I didn't think it would be this difficult." He stares at the floor for a second. "I can't do much now, tonight, but I'm going to work out a way of solving this, Gem, OK?"

I look at him and nod. I believe him. It's a good feeling. "We can do that together."

He smiles at me and nods and puts his arm around my shoulder.

"I'm OK now," I say. "Let's go back."

"I still want to know what Minxie said," says Joe and I follow him back to our table.

The spilled drink has been cleared up and the waitress is writing down our orders. A new bubble bottle is sitting at my place. I pick up a menu and stare at it. I was starving before but now I'm not sure I can eat a thing.

Joe doesn't sit with Lexi. He sits next to me. There's an odd atmosphere around the table. I'm not sure if it's because of what Minxie said or something else.

"Right, have you finally decided?" he says. "I'm starving."

"Don't get irritated with me," says Lexi. "It's not my fault the waitress doesn't know *exactly* what's in the salad dressing."

Joe breathes deeply and I'm pretty sure there is a new problem. They must have started ordering before Joe came to find me.

Minxie looks just the same as before. She's not red or bothered or fidgety. She's just picking her nails, sipping her drink.

I pretend I'm deep in thought, trying to make a decision. When it's my turn to order, I choose a simple burger but I have no idea how I'm going to eat it.

Chapter Thirty

We race through dinner and leave straight away. Joe is quiet. He puts the radio on.

"I'm sorry I spilled my drink," I say.

"Doesn't matter two hoots, Gem," he says. "I'm angry with the two of them, not you." He spins round to look at me. "You know that, don't you? Please don't think this is about you." And I nod because I know it.

"Mum says that. The two hoots thing," I say, looking at him. I want to try to cheer him up. "She always says things don't matter two hoots."

Joe smiles and nods. "We got that saying from Gran, I think."

"It's an odd saying."

"Yep," says Joe. "And sometimes things *do* matter."

The sun is going down, just a deep orange slither

dipped behind the skyline. We drive down the country lanes, the fields covered in the dusky light. Joe turns down the radio.

"So ... what did Minxie say to upset you?"

I fiddle with the straps of my bag. "She just said a strange thing."

"Which was...?" says Joe.

We pass the train station. There are two people on a bench outside, with suitcases. I wonder if they have been on a cruise, like Mum. I don't really feel like talking about Minxie now, especially after dinner went a bit wrong.

"Please, Gemma," says Joe. "I hated seeing you so upset." He waits, glances at me. "Was she unkind? Did she tease you?"

"No!" I say. "No, nothing like that." And then I feel I *have* to tell Joe or he might think Minxie has been mean and as much as I dislike her, that wouldn't be fair. And Joe *did* say he would help to solve it all. "She said everyone was waiting to see me play tennis. That it was in my blood." We slow up at the level crossing but the barriers stay up and we rattle over the tracks. "She said she wasn't meant to say anything. That no one is meant to." I glance at him, wait for him to say something, but he just blinks and twists his mouth a little.

We drive along in silence. The news comes on the radio. It's about a hurricane that's swept across Louisiana. Joe turns it off. The sun disappears, the golden glow gone from the sky.

"What does she mean?" I ask him. "And why is everyone so surprised I haven't played before?"

Joe laughs a little. "You can now," he says. "You're smashing it, Gem! Smash, it's a tennis shot. Get it?" He laughs, turns to me as if he's hoping I will laugh too, make everything lighter. I'm not in the mood to laugh. I want to find out more, break the piñata and see the secrets spill out.

"Do they mean *you*?" I ask. "Is it because *you* are so good at tennis, they think I'm going to be some sort of whizz-kid player?"

He starts to say something but stops, takes a breath, taps the steering wheel.

We pull on to his drive. Carrot Cake is waiting by the front door. Joe turns the engine off and we sit for a minute watching him.

"You need to talk to your mum, Gem," he says.

"Oh," I say.

"It's only right that she tells you things, not me."

"Oh." I'm about to say, "Tells me *what* things," but

I stop myself. I don't want to push it. I don't want to make Joe unhappy.

"I'm sorry it's confusing," he says. "I said I'd help to solve things and I will, I promise. We'll phone her tomorrow, OK?"

"OK."

"She's off the ship on some island today. I texted her earlier to let her know how Gran's getting on with the carers. She told me they're all riding donkeys up a hill to a taverna."

We both smile and undo our seat belts.

"Poor donkeys," I say.

"Maybe she'll share one with Jerry," says Joe. "As he's her boyfriend."

"He is *not*!"

Joe smiles and we both climb out of the car. He leans down to tickle Carrot Cake. "Let's feed you, waste of space," he says as he puts the key in the door.

I lie awake, the moonlight gushing into the room. I think about Mum and talking to her tomorrow.

It's only right that she tells you things.

What things? What has Mum never told me?

I used to think Mum and I told each other everything but the longer I'm here and the more I'm trying to find out about the past and the fallout, the more I realize how *much* she has kept hidden.

She has never told me anything about the fallout.

Or my dad.

I pick up the little notebook by my bed. Mark off the days. It's the first time I've thought of the little tally chart since I made it. Five lines, five days. Nearly a week.

I hear Joe come up to bed. He calls out gently, "Night, Gem."

I call back, "Night, Joe."

He knocks softly and opens the door. "Are you OK?"

I close the notebook super fast. I'd hate Joe to see the chart.

"Yep."

"Gem," he says.

"Yep."

"Thanks for being understanding today. I know this must be hard."

"Yep. OK."

"Night, lovely girl."

"Night, Joe."

He closes the door and I hear him use the bathroom and go to his room.

I sit up, hug my knees.

I don't know what he means. How have I been "understanding"? Does he mean about him and Lexi falling out? Or for not pushing him to answer my questions? I don't get it. Why wouldn't he just admit the tennis thing was because of him? Why the big problem with it all?

And then it hits me.

Smack.

The things Mum and I have *never* talked about?

It must be the same things everyone here is not *allowed* to talk about.

The fallout and my dad must be linked. Maybe my dad is the *reason* for the fallout.

It's not Joe who I take after, not Joe who I share the magic tennis genes with.

It's my dad.

My dad is a tennis player. He must be. That's where it comes from. My father. I get out of bed and pace up and down the room, my mind racing. All these people must know that my father is an amazing tennis player and that's why they all thought I'd be good. That's why Mum was so cross I was playing. That was the horrid silence when she heard about the new kit Joe had bought me. That's why Joe said it was only right that Mum tell me things. This is all to do with my dad.

I sit on the bed and try to make a picture in my mind of my dad. He is on a tennis court, slamming serves down, chasing shots, whacking volleys.

The thoughts tumble.

The fallout, the things people aren't meant to say, the thing that's in my blood. The wedding day; the efforts to make a fresh start. Maybe that was because my dad was not involved, out of the way, so they wanted to patch things up. I try hard to remember more, to take the few brief things I can remember and dig deeper. But all I can think of is the pink bathroom and the nasty bride and the flowers and now, something new.

Grass. Rolling over grass down a sloping bank, laughing as I do it.

Chapter Thirty-one

"Really thought this would work," says Joe. Smoke is billowing from the pan. "How hard can pancakes be?" He swears as the next one burns.

"These look OK," I say, turning over the few on the pile.

"All yours, Gem!" says Joe, passing me the spatula and wafting the burnt smell away with a tea towel. "I'm sorry I can't take you to tennis today. Are you sure you're OK going with Lexi?"

"Of course," I say.

I'm not OK with it. I really don't want to go with her, especially after last night. Things were really odd when we all said goodbye.

"These Friday meetings are important and I need to get the seven-thirty train. Lexi should be here very soon."

"I'm fine to wait on my own," I say. But he shakes his head.

"No need," he says. His phone rings. "I bet this is her, saying she's running late." He answers it. "Hey, Carrie... How's life on the ocean?"

I almost wish it *was* Lexi calling, not Mum. It's odd because I feel nervous about talking to her. I've never ever in my life felt nervous talking to Mum.

Joe passes me the phone and says, "I'm going to get changed." I nod and wait until he's gone.

"Hi, Gem," says Mum. She sounds sleepy. "I thought I'd call early to catch you. It's super late here. I'm just about to go to bed! We've been watching movies all night. How are you, darling?"

I take a deep breath, pick at the burnt edge of a pancake.

"Fine." It comes out sharp, irritated.

"OK... How's things? Are you having fun?"

"Yep."

We are quiet, with just the crackle of distant cruise-line air. She's phoned for a normal, quick chat. She can tell I'm wound up. Mum always knows how I'm feeling. Even when we are thousands of miles apart.

"I miss you," she says. "A month is too long to be away."

I make a sort of "mmmm" sound, like I'm not agreeing or disagreeing.

"What's up, Gem?" she says.

I hesitate for a moment, sweep some crumbs away. And then I say, "Joe says you need to tell me things."

Silence. Then Mum's breath, deep and sighing. "What's this about, Gem?"

"Everyone seems to know stuff that I don't. About me. Nothing makes sense. I need to know more about the past, why you and Gran and Joe fell out." I pause. Silence. So I keep going. "And I want to know about my dad too."

Mum breathes in fast, a gulp of air and then she is quiet. Carrot Cake rubs himself round my legs. He calms me. I wait.

"Wow," she says. "That's a lot, Gem. I didn't want you to go away and be wrapped up in all this worry."

"Well," I blurt, "I am. I want to find out. I want to know these things. Your friends say I'm growing up. You need to see it too."

"I do!" she says. "I really do, Gem. But I think we should talk about this when I'm home."

"I want to talk about it all now," I reply. Silence again and then I hear voices in the room. "Who's that with you?"

"Jerry. Just Jerry. He's brought me some juice."

"Oh, goody for you," I say, flicking a bit of burnt pancake across the worktop. "I want to know the truth about my life and you're more worried about your boyfriend Jerry."

"He's not my boyfriend. You know that!"

"Joe thinks he is."

"Yes, well, Joe doesn't know everything."

"He knows a lot. And he says *you* need to tell me stuff."

"Oh, did he now?"

I'm quiet. Joe's phone pings several times as if someone is texting. I look at the screen. There are messages from Minxie, lots of them. When I put the phone back to my ear, I can hear Mum in the background telling Jerry that she'll see him in the morning.

"Gemma," she says. "I've tried to do the right thing."

"What does everyone mean?" I say. "Tennis is *in my blood*. Was my dad a tennis player, is that why? Was he the reason everyone fell out? He must be."

"We'll talk about this when I see you," she says. I can hear her voice tremble a little, as if the tears are brewing. "I know I've made mistakes, Gem, I know I have. I should have been more honest from the start but I don't want to do this over the phone, OK?"

I'm not sure what to say. It does feel odd talking about this when I'm not with her. We are both quiet. The phone pings again, over and over.

Joe comes back in, all smart in a blue suit with a shiny striped tie.

"How was the donkey ride?" he shouts, loud enough that Mum hears.

Mum laughs a bit. I can tell she's glad to talk about something silly, easy. "I fell off," she says. "Got a mighty bruise on my left hip."

I smile a tiny smile.

"I've got to go now, Gem," says Mum. "Can we speak over the weekend and then when I'm home we can discuss everything? Let me just gather my thoughts, OK?"

Gather my thoughts. Mum uses that expression a lot. Like her thoughts are all one big, jumbled mess.

Joe tips biscuits in Carrot Cake's bowl and looks at his watch. He needs to leave.

"OK," I say. I feel like I've pushed enough. "Speak at the weekend."

"Love you, Gem," says Mum.

I think of her slipping off the donkey, lying in a big heap with a hurt hip. "Love you too, Mum." I press the end button and pass Joe his phone. I pull on my tracksuit top, zipping it right up so I can nestle into it.

"Poor donkey," says Joe. I smile at him and he smiles back, that left twist of the mouth right there, just like Mum.

His phone pings again.

"I think someone was texting you," I say. I don't say it was Minxie because I'm not sure I should have looked.

He looks at the phone, scrolls down, rakes his hand through his hair. And then he makes a call. I can hear the ringing sound.

"Hey, Minx, you OK? ... Right... She said what ... that I'd have to take you? The gym? ... She's gone to *the gym*?" He looks at his watch, sighs. "No, don't call your dad. It's fine... Yes, she did know... Have you had some breakfast? ... OK. It's fine... No, you're not missing tennis. I'll get you... OK. Stop it, Minx, it's fine... You did the right thing... Text your mum and tell her I'm getting you... I'll be there soon. OK? Bye, Minx."

Joe ends the call and looks up at the ceiling, makes a face as if he's thinking hard. And then he makes another call. He heads into his office and I just hear a few words.

"...Really sorry ... do you mind delaying until ten? ... Someone's let me down..."

I run upstairs and quickly get ready. None of this would have happened if I wasn't here. I grab my tennis kit and my racket and run back downstairs. Joe is on the phone, madly texting.

"Your lunch, Gem," says Joe, not looking up from his phone. "It's in the fridge." And I feel this absolute pang of something for Joe. He has all this to deal with and he's *still* made me lunch, still thought about me first. I run and get it.

"OK?" he says.

"Yep," I say, shoving the lunch in my bag. "I'm really sorry. If I wasn't here you wouldn't have to sort all of this out."

Joe puts his arm around me and says, "You coming to stay is the *best* thing that's happened all year, OK?"

I nod and smile and we go out to the car, Carrot Cake watching us from the hallway, his paws neatly side by side, his tail curled round in front.

Chapter
Thirty-two

I don't recognize the journey to Lexi's. We came from the shopping centre last time and that feels a long time ago. We go on a long straight road with no trees and a big farm with cows in the field.

"I'm sorry about your early train," I say.

"It's OK, Gem, I've sorted it."

"Did Lexi forget she was taking us both today?"

"Um ... did Lexi forget?" He makes a fake thinking sound and taps the steering wheel. "No, I think Lexi absolutely knew and she wanted to make things a little bit tricky. I don't mind her making things tricky for me, but not for Minxie."

"I get that," I say.

It's not long before we pull up at Lexi's cottage.

"Will you get her, Gem?" asks Joe. "I just need to

make another call." I nod and jump out and walk up the path, knock on the door. After a minute, Minxie appears. She doesn't say a word to me. I think she might have been crying. She just pulls the door behind her and runs down the path to the car.

It's odd then because Minxie gets straight in the front seat. She doesn't even check if that's OK. My bag is there and she picks it up and plonks it on the back seat. I open the door and shuffle over all the balls and rackets and get in. It's cramped in the back and it's hard to find the seat belt. I stare at Minxie's head and feel a shot of anger or jealousy. I'm not sure which. Joe's *my* uncle. Mine. I'm living with him right now. Surely that means *I* go in the front seat and she goes in the back.

Joe finishes his call and pulls off.

Minxie fiddles with the radio, plugs in her phone as if this is something she's done lots of times before.

"No music right now, thanks, Minxie," says Joe. She tuts and takes her phone out again and mutters something about Joe being boring. He ignores her. I want to shout at her for speaking to him like that, tell her that this whole morning is a mess because he had to pick *her* up and take us both to tennis. But I know I can't do that so I just slump down and stare out of the window as the fields flash by, watch the cows bent down, feeding.

"Was your mum OK this morning?" asks Joe.

"Not really," says Minxie. "But not as bad as last night when we got home. You were *not* in her good books for not phoning her back." She mimics her then and she gets Lexi's voice so right that it's hard not to smile. She rattles away so fast. "*Joe never calls when he says he will, Joe doesn't know how hard it is...* You know what she's like." Then she says a few things about her mum that really aren't very nice and I don't want to smile about it any more.

"That's enough now," says Joe, raising his left hand in a sort of stop sign.

"OK," says Minxie, tossing her hair over her shoulder. She stares out of the window. We rumble over the bridge that crosses the river.

"I'm just pleased you called me," says Joe. "And you're coming to tennis."

"I still wanna give it up," says Minxie.

Joe stops at the junction and says, "That's something I really can't get involved with."

"You could try," says Minxie and she turns to him, laughing. "You could challenge my dad to a duel. You know, like in the medieval days."

"Stop it, Minx!" says Joe but he can't help but smile as Minx describes her dad and Joe turning up on horseback, with jousting swords, Carrot Cake up front as Joe's mascot.

For a bit, I feel totally out of place, rammed in the back of Joe's car, listening to them. They have lots of stuff to remember and things they have shared.

Joe is my uncle. All I have are a couple of memories from long ago and the things that have happened since Saturday when Mum flew away to the other side of the world.

But that's a good place to start.

Chapter
Thirty-three

We pull up at the club. Minxie thanks Joe and goes into the clubhouse.

Sophie's car is next to us. Bradley is in the back, curled over, his face buried. Sophie gets out and bends down next to Joe's open window.

"Mungo is going back to his owner today," she says in a quiet voice, almost a whisper. "It's been a tough morning."

Joe nods and thinks for a moment and then he opens the car door and gets out and climbs into the back seat of Sophie's car. I can just see from where I'm sitting. He tugs Bradley into him and I hear the tears through the open window. I grab my things and get out and head for the clubhouse.

Sophie comes too and sits with me on the bench

outside, looking out at the court, the morning sun warming us.

"Poor Bradley," I mutter.

"Yes, it's not easy," says Sophie. She rustles in her bag for her sunglasses.

"I'd love a cat," I say. "Or a dog."

"One day," says Sophie, slipping the glasses on. "It has to be the right time."

I nod. "Gran has dogs. I'm meeting them tomorrow for the first time!"

"Fab," says Sophie.

Bradley gets out of the car, wiping his eyes, looks up for his mum. Sophie raises one hand and smiles. "He's going for a sleepover later, after tennis, with his friend. I thought that was the best plan."

"It must be really hard. Mungo's such a lovely cat."

Sophie turns to look at me. "I just need to check with you, Gem," she says. "You'll be with me later when Mungo goes. Is that OK?"

"Of course," I say, although I feel a little sick at the thought of it.

"We'll make flapjacks," says Sophie. "Good plan?"

"Great."

Bradley runs past us into the clubhouse. Joe gives

us a wave and thumbs up and gets back in his car and drives away.

It's good to hit the ball. I feel a bit better now I've said something to Mum, thrown it out there. It feels like the truth will have to come out now, that I'll find a way to mend things, however hard that might be.

"You're on fire today!" says Sarah.

We are volleying to each other, the ball bouncing from one racket to the other without touching the ground. We make twelve. It's coming together, the feeling of moving to the ball, attacking the shot, planning where it's going to land. It's like athletics and chess, all mixed up together. Moving but always thinking. Running and planning at the same time. I wonder if my dad was good at volleys.

Flori stands by the side, watching us. She is paired with Minxie but Minxie has disappeared into the clubhouse.

Jake arrives on his bike, his racket slung over his shoulder. He comes on to court followed by the twins.

"Jake," calls Pam. "Can you try volleying with Flori? I've no idea where Minxie's gone."

Flori peels herself away from the back netting as if Velcro is holding her there. Jake shows her what to do.

"Racket up," he says. "Come on, it won't hurt you."

Minxie comes out of the clubhouse, her hair twisted in a clever little knot at the back.

"Oh, coming!" she calls. "Sorry to have left you, Flori!"

Flori glares at her and pulls her lips tight.

"Ooh, can I have a go?" says Minxie.

"You hit with Flori," says Jake. "She's getting the hang of it now." He leaves to work with Raj and Max, Minxie watching him with a "that wasn't what I meant" look on her face.

We practise all the shots. Ball after ball. Forehands are my favourite. A good strong forehand and then a dash into the net for a volley. Pam teaches us how to smash. She loops the ball high and tells us to come down hard on it from overhead, like a serve. I love it. Pointing with one hand up at the ball, following it in the air, connecting hard with the strings and banging it down on to the court.

"There you go, Joe," I whisper to myself, with a smile. "I'm *totally* smashing it."

"How can you be so good *so soon*?" says Flori, watching the ball sail over her head. "I can't even *watch* it long enough."

"I'm learning," I shout. "Just like you."

"This one, Flori!" yells Pam. She hoists up an easy ball. Flori points at it, swings her racket and misses completely, her body spinning with the effort. We both giggle and when Pam says it's time for lunch, Flori collapses with relief.

Chapter Thirty-four

We fetch our packed lunches from the clubhouse. I go to the loo first and when I come out, just my bag is waiting. Minxie is rummaging in hers, tipping things out. She mutters a bad word and gets out her phone, presses buttons.

"Mum, I've got nothing to eat. I'm starving." And then she hangs up and I realize she was leaving a message. She slumps down on the bench, stares out at the courts, her mouth pinched, breathing fast.

I get my lunch and open it. It's massive, of course.

"Share mine," I say.

Minxie slants her eyes at me. "It's fine," she says.

"No, honestly, Joe puts more in than I can *ever* eat."

She lets out a huff of air and allows herself a tiny smile.

I want to just share the food and leave. I unzip the lunch box. There are two huge rolls, crisps, a yoghurt drink and a biscuit. I start to lay it out. Minxie shifts on the bench, tilts her head back and sighs.

"I'm meant to say sorry for upsetting you last night," she says.

I keep sorting the lunch, don't look up.

"Sorry," she says, in a totally fake way. It's the same voice I've heard her use for "laters" or "whatever".

I put her roll on the lid of the lunch box.

"Are you not going to say anything?" she says, taking one of the crisps that I've tipped out for her.

"I'm not sure why you've said it," I say. "You don't mean it."

Raj comes in then to fill his water bottle. She waits for him, glances round the room as if a little lost for what to say, surprised at my answer. Raj scuttles out, yelling to Bradley to meet him on court one.

"Well," says Minxie. "I sort of do. If I don't, then *apparently*..." she stops, pulls a face, mimicks Lexi and gets it spot on, "I'm absolutely not going to any sleepovers or parties for two weeks."

I look at her and smile a little and she actually smiles back.

I pick up my roll. I want to go outside with Flori and Sarah but it would feel a bit strange just walking out now.

"Anyway, Joe asked me," says Minxie. "And I'll do it for Joe." She picks up her roll and bites into it. "Thanks for this."

I nod, take a crisp. "I'm actually quite pleased you *did* say it, the thing in the pub I mean."

She looks at me, doesn't say anything.

"There are lots of things I don't know about my family and it's good to feel like I'm finding out stuff."

She nods.

"I don't know anything about my dad."

She chews and stares outside. "What *nothing*?"

"Zip," I say.

It feels strangely OK to ask Minxie more. I want to ask her about what she said last night but Flori rushes in, orange juice all down her T-shirt.

"Look at me!" she says. "Sarah knocked it right out of my hand."

Sarah follows her in. "I'll help rinse it out," she says. "And I have a spare you can borrow." They scuttle off to the loos, giggling.

The questions I have for Minxie, the strange ease I felt in talking to her, they've both disappeared, like they've been smashed off the court.

"That's too cold!" shrieks Flori from the loo.

Minxie sighs as if she can't bear to hear them. She picks up the half strip of biscuit I shared with her and takes it outside. I watch her as she walks over to the sunny grass and sits down and eats. Part of me wants to follow her out, see if I can get our chat back on track, find out what she knows. But I'm not sure she will tell me much and, to be honest, I'm really not sure I want to find out the truth from Minxie.

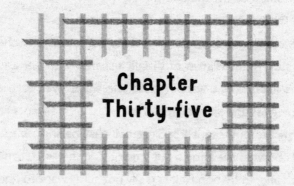

Chapter
Thirty-five

After lunch, Pam splits us into groups to play a game. She puts me with Flori which I'm fine about because I like Flori but it's also hard because Flori doesn't move her feet. She only tries to hit the balls that land right in front of her and then she misses most of them.

"Remember to shout out the score at the start of each point," says Jake. "Knowing the score is really important. You'll lose track otherwise."

Flori starts serving which is a disaster because even doing it underarm, she can't get it over the net. We are playing the twins. I have no idea why Pam put them together. They swap sides each time, which they aren't meant to. They take turns to serve one point at a time, which isn't the rules. They fall out and start using the rackets like weapons. Pam has to come and split them up and stand by the net and watch.

One game each and my turn to serve.

"Last game of the day!" shouts Pam to both courts.

Last game. Winner of this game wins.

We lose the first point – Finlay did a lucky return.

"Love–fifteen," I call out.

We lose the second point as Flori misses the ball and hits herself instead.

"Love–thirty."

The other group finish their game and stand by the back net watching. It makes me flustered, them all being there. I get my serve in but hit a forehand way out of court, so far it hits the back netting. I can't remember what number comes next.

"What's the score?" I ask Flori. She is the super scorer. She got it all straight away.

"Love–forty."

We swap sides and I get the balls ready for the next point. I have to tell Flori where to stand when I serve. She is putting her headband back on, fiddling with the T-shirt Sarah's lent her.

"What's the score?" shouts Max.

"Love–forty," I shout, nice and clear like Jake and Pam told us to do.

"Three game points!" yells Raj.

I don't want to lose the game. I want to win it. I get ready to serve, think about my dad, bouncing the balls, planning his shots. I serve the ball hard and Max can't even get a racket to it. I serve two more really strong points and put a volley away.

"Deuce," calls Flori.

I serve again. Finlay sends it back but it is a high, loopy shot. It's a perfect smash for Flori. She watches it, puts her hand up to point at it like Pam showed us. And then waves the racket through the air and misses the ball. I race over, hit it just before it touches the ground and tap it back over. Point won.

"Great chase," shouts Jake.

"Our advantage," says Flori.

I serve again. Max returns it. It comes to Flori, right in front of her. I take in a breath, wait for her to miss it but she hits it. She volleys it. It comes off the frame, not the strings but it sails over the net at the most amazing angle.

"Genius shot!" shouts Pam.

Flori screeches with excitement.

"Must be the lucky T-shirt," shouts Sarah.

We win the game.

It's such a good feeling.

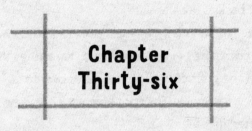

Chapter
Thirty-six

Pam calls us all together. "It's been a great first week, you've all worked so hard. I'm afraid you only have me next week. Jake is off to a training camp so he can't be with us."

Everyone looks disappointed.

"It's been a blast," says Jake. "Best of luck with next Friday's tournament." He opens up his rucksack and passes out packets of pastilles. Finlay and Max rush to grab theirs.

"Wicked," says Raj.

Minxie takes her packet with a small smile but looks at them as if she has totally outgrown sweets and she's not sure what they are. A car beeps its horn. Bradley looks round and waves to his friend.

"I'm going on a sleepover!" he says but no one hears.

"Have fun, Brad," I say, and he turns and smiles.

Flori and Sarah run into the clubhouse to swap the T-shirt back.

"See you Monday, Gemma!" yells Sarah and I wave at them both. The twins run off court. Raj bashes the ball against the practice wall. Minxie heads over to Lexi's car.

I look for Sophie. She's not here yet. I hope she hasn't forgotten me.

"Gemma," says Jake. I look round at him. He picks up the last few balls and turns the winder to lower the net. "Keep playing, won't you?" I nod, tap my racket on the ground. "You'll improve fast. You've got natural talent." He throws the balls towards the basket. One misses and rolls away. I pick it up and roll it in my hands.

"It's my dad," I say. "He played." Jake nods as if he knows and then he wheels the basket away and leaves the court, one hand waving high.

It's so odd. I've said something *out loud* about my dad. Maybe soon, I'll know more about him. Not just that he plays tennis. Maybe I'll know what movies he likes and his favourite food. I can say things like "Oh, my dad loves cheese", or "Oh, my dad drives a car like that" and "Oh yes, my dad's been to Spain".

Jake knows my dad was a good tennis player. Minxie

knows. That's why she said it was "in my blood". It seems everyone knows and that's what Minxie meant when she said the whole tennis club had been talking about me but no one was allowed to say anything. Now I need to work out if it's linked to the great family fallout. We go to Gran's tomorrow. Maybe Gran will help me to discover more.

Sophie's car pulls up. She jumps out, waves at me and calls, "I just need to talk to Pam." I wave back.

I still have the ball in my hand. I hit it against the wall, over and over, the blister on my right hand rubbing and sore but I really don't care.

Chapter Thirty-seven

We are stirring the oats and syrup when there is a knock at the door.

"Keep stirring, Gem," says Sophie. "I won't be long."

She opens the front door. I peep round, watching from the kitchen. There is an elderly lady leaning on a stick and a younger woman who I think is her daughter.

Sophie takes them into the lounge. I hear bits of chat.

So grateful ... thought he'd run away.

Microchipped now ... my son is very fond of him.

Mum's been in hospital for a long while...

Oh, he's actually called Marmaduke ... how lovely.

We looked everywhere ... so thrilled to find him.

Any problems just call me ... we would always take care of him.

Sophie heads for Mungo's room. I follow to see if

I can help. Mungo is fast asleep.

"If you can just hold the carrier door open," says Sophie, gently lifting him. I hold the wire door while Sophie carefully tucks Mungo inside. He doesn't want to go in. He meows and tries to back up.

"Good job Bradley isn't here," mutters Sophie, fastening the catch and stroking Mungo's nose through the bars. She turns and looks at me. "It's not normally this hard. He's called Marmaduke."

"Mungo suits him better," I say, and I reach through the bars and tickle his head.

We take him into the hall. The ladies come out of the lounge and say thanks to Sophie as she hands over the carrier. As they walk away down the path, Mungo looks back at us through the bars. The old lady struggles to get into the car, wincing as she lifts her legs in.

Bobby sits by the front door, watching.

"Any problems, just call me," shouts Sophie. "You have my number, yes?" The younger lady waves and says they do. "My son," shouts Sophie. "He really loves him." She gulps a little and sniffs hard, picks up Bobby and nestles into his neck.

They drive away and we head back to the kitchen.

"Right, Gem," says Sophie. "Come on, flapjacks!"

We finish the baking and spend time in the garden. Joe arrives and we sit outside with tea and the flapjacks.

"What are you up to this weekend?" asks Sophie.

Joe sips his tea. "Well, we're off to Mum's tomorrow."

"Oh yes, you'll meet the dogs, Gem!" says Sophie, and I nod hard and smile.

"I'm excited," I say.

"But tonight," says Joe, "I've got to take a special lady out for the meal of her choice to make up for last night."

Sophie stretches back in the sunshine and looks at him. "Wow, lucky Lexi, where are you off to?"

Joe tips his mug back and is about to tell her when Sophie dives forward in her chair. "Let me have Gemma. Oh Gem, stay with me tonight!"

I'm nodding and smiling. I'd much rather be with Sophie than out with Lexi again.

Joe stares at Sophie and shakes his head. "No chance. The very lovely lady *is* Gemma. Just you and me tonight, Gem."

I'm so relieved the others aren't coming.

"Oh," says Sophie, smiling. "*Much* better!"

Joe glances at his watch. "We better get going." We stand up and walk through to the hall. I pick up my bag.

"Ooh, almost forgot," says Sophie and she dashes back to the kitchen.

"What food do you feel like, Gem?" asks Joe, one hand tugging his floppy fringe. "Maybe we could see a movie too?"

"I don't know," I say. Sophie returns and hands me a Tupperware full of flapjack.

I turn to Joe. "Can Sophie come with us?"

"Um," says Joe, shoving his hands in his pockets.

"Oh gosh, no," says Sophie, sweeping away a cobweb from over the doorway. "Wouldn't dream of it."

It's a bit funny now. We are all very quiet. It's like I've said the wrong thing. And then Joe turns to Sophie and says, "Why don't you? Come on. It's only a movie and a bite to eat."

She picks up her mail and sifts through the envelopes. "No, it's fine, lots to do here."

He bends down a little, looks for her eyes. "Come on. You've had a tough day with Bradley upset and Mungo leaving. It's just a bite to eat."

"Please," I say.

She stares at him, smiles at me. "OK. Why not? I'll grab my bag."

We wait while she gets her things and locks the door

and then we walk down the path and I hear her say to Joe, "She won't like it."

And I'm pretty sure she must mean Lexi.

Chapter
Thirty-eight

We eat Chinese food in a restaurant. Joe orders the banquet for four. There is so much food that I feel a bit odd, like I can't really eat now. There are lots of things I haven't tried before. Mum and I only have a few dishes with our takeouts and we spend ages choosing them.

"You OK, Gem?" says Joe.

"Yep."

"Do you like Chinese?"

"I love it," I say. "Mum and I sometimes have it. Or curry. For our last Friday of the month takeout night."

"Sounds great," says Joe, taking a giant prawn cracker and breaking it in two.

"Yep. It's a big night. We choose our dishes and then Mum gets the money…"

I stop there. I don't want to tell them that she gets

the money from the shoebox she keeps under the bed. Mum doesn't even know *I* know about that.

"We order it from one of the local takeaways," I say. "They're all really good."

Joe nods. He takes a few spring rolls, so I do the same.

"We love takeout Friday. Mum and I make a real thing of it, lay the table all pretty and keep a diary of how good it is and rate all the dishes out of ten. At the moment, the curry house is ahead. Their butter chicken is *the* best."

Joe is staring at me, chewing slowly.

"What?" I ask. "Is it all down my chin?"

"No, no," says Joe, reaching for the dumplings. "I was just thinking about your mum, that's all. She makes things special, doesn't she?"

I nod. She does.

"I think it sounds a fab idea!" says Sophie. "I might start that with Bradley."

We finish up the food, scrape out the dishes. I think I eat all the sweet and sour chicken, every bit.

It's odd because the banquet was for four but we've nearly eaten everything. There is only a bit of egg fried rice left. Joe asks for the bill and I ask if they are going to eat it. They both say no. They're talking about one of Sophie's clients and how she is chasing them for payment.

I like it when they chat like that. It's like a different world that I know nothing about.

I lift up the bowl and scrape out the last bit. Mum and I never leave a thing. Not one grain. It's called the "Gembamumba clean up". I chase the last scrap of egg round the dish. Joe and Sophie's words flow over me, and I have a pang to be with Mum. To see her, hug her and tell her stuff.

The cinema is near the big sports shop where me and Joe bought my new gear. The shop is shut but I can see the rackets hanging on the wall and the trainers in the middle aisles. It seems ages ago since we were there. Not just five days. The five days makes me think about the tally chart. I'm not going to finish it. I don't need to count the days any more. Not now.

The movie is about a superhero. She flies faster than sound. Her boyfriend can lift up lorries. Joe keeps looking at me during the kissing scenes, all concerned as if I've never seen two people kiss. One kiss goes on for ages and Joe covers my eyes. Sophie throws popcorn at him to stop but it lands all over the back of the guy sitting in front of us and we have to carefully pick it off his woollen jumper.

On the way home, we can't stop laughing.

"I cannot believe the poor guy didn't feel it!" says Sophie. "And *you* ate it, Joe," laughs Sophie. "Right off his jumper."

We pull up at traffic lights. It is a big, wide road with two lanes. We are laughing so much that Joe is bent over the steering wheel. And then he looks up and stops laughing.

The traffic lights are still on red but the car next to us is revving its engine hard. Joe looks at the driver.

"Oh ##$$%," he says. Mum hates that word.

Sophie and I look over. It's Lexi. She stares at Joe, then at Sophie. Sophie's laughter dries up and she looks out of the other window. I kind of raise my hand to wave but Lexi doesn't see me. The lights change and we pull away. Lexi's car sits for a moment, quite still and then as I look behind me, I see her pull off, turning a different way.

Nothing seems funny any more. Joe turns on the radio and the DJ helps to fill the air. We drive through the tunnel of trees and across the level crossing. The DJ talks about some car festival happening in town and then he plays music. Joe taps his fingers on the steering wheel but I can tell he's not feeling great.

"You excited to see your gran tomorrow, Gem?" asks Sophie, looking round at me from the front seat.

"Yep," I say.

"What time are you leaving?" she asks Joe. I think she wants to get him talking, make him feel better.

"Morning sometime," he says.

We pull up at Sophie's house. Bobby is by the front door.

"Thanks for a great evening," says Sophie as she climbs out. "Have fun tomorrow. Sorry if, you know, us laughing should be a problem."

Joe shakes his head. "Of course not," he says and then he watches Sophie as she lets herself into her house, Bobby wrapped around her ankles. She closes the door and still Joe sits watching. The lights come on, Sophie pulls the lounge curtains across and we drive slowly away.

Chapter Thirty-nine

It's late when we get home but Joe asks if I want to watch some TV. Joe has a beer and I have ice cream. The adverts come on. There is a man changing a baby's nappy. He has a peg on his nose.

"It's so sad about Bradley's dad," I say.

"It's tragic about Bradley's dad," says Joe. "Chris was a great guy."

The TV advert man takes the peg off his nose. Some wonderful new spray has taken the smell away.

Joe takes a swig of his beer and turns the volume down.

"Did you have a good chat with your mum this morning?"

I nod. We both stare back at the screen. It's an advert for washing powder. There is a row of mucky rugby players. One girl has mud literally everywhere.

"Sort of," I say. "She wants to tell me everything when I see her but she did say we'd talk more at the weekend."

"OK," says Joe. "That makes sense."

"Nothing really makes sense."

We both watch the girl throw herself over the line with the ball, slipping in the pool of mud. Then she's at home, being hosed down. A big box of washing powder flashes on to the screen.

"He was a tennis player, my dad, wasn't he?"

Joe leans forward on the sofa and turns the TV off. I've said such a big thing but it's odd because I'd quite like to have seen the girl after the washing powder worked its magic.

"I've no idea, Gemma," he says. "He might have been."

"You know he played tennis. Everyone does. It's this 'in your blood' thing. It's not you, is it, it's my dad? Problems with my dad led to this big family fallout. That's why I don't see any of you, or him."

Joe moves to sit on the coffee table, facing me.

"Now just hold on, Gem. We know nothing about your dad. Nothing. Zip. Your mum came back from America and wouldn't tell any of us a thing. It was part of the problem. She came back and told us she was having a baby but nothing else." He sips his beer again. "But I know about you now, Gemma. Your mum did a great job with you. You're a fab young lady and it's magical for me to spend this time with you. I never thought your mum would quite forgive us enough for this to happen."

He looks down, taps the bottle, bites his lip. I stare at him. Why would Mum need to *forgive* them? I shake my head a little, try to make the thoughts fall into place.

"Was the fallout because of my dad, because of Mum getting pregnant, because of *me*?"

"NO!" He shouts it, looks almost afraid I should think that. "It was nothing to do with that. We loved you from the very start."

"*Why* then?"

Joe stares at me. I know he wants to tell me more. "We all made mistakes. Especially me. Having this chance now, to be with you, Gemma, to build a relationship. That means the world to me."

And then there is a loud knocking at the front door. It makes us both jump a little. It's very late for someone to be coming round.

We sit quietly for a second. Joe puts his beer down.

"I think I know who this is," he says. "Let's make sure you and your mum speak tomorrow, OK?" I nod. He pats me on the knee and gives me a little smile, the one that twists to the side and reminds me of Mum. "I'm sorry, Gemma. I might be a while."

He gets up to answer the door. I gather my things and dash upstairs and after a few minutes I hear Lexi's voice and her heels pounding across the hall floor.

I try to hear and I try not to hear. I leave my bedroom door open and catch the voices drifting upstairs.

... just wanted an evening with Gemma...

... how come Sophie was there...

... always some excuse...

... if you wanted her there, why didn't you want me there...

... drop anything for Sophie...

... this isn't working out...

And then the front door slams shut. I hear Lexi's car drive away, the tyres squealing. And then Joe flicks on the TV and even though I really feel like watching TV again, I stay in my room.

I think Joe was close to telling me more. If we'd just had a few more minutes I might have found out the truth. I'm getting closer to it. I'm pretty sure my mum got pregnant in America. My dad might be from *America*.

There's no way I can sleep now – I get out my phone and message the girls.

Gemma: Anyone awake?

Surinder: 👍 OMG there's this family in the next door tent and the dad snores soooooo loud. I can't wait to get home to brick walls.

Jess: me too awake I mean

Gemma: hows the puppy?

Jess: So cute. He chased that same cat. It ran up a tree and got stuck there. Dad had to get a ladder to rescue it.

Surinder: There's a pool at the campsite. I'm wearing a verruca sock. So unfair.

Gemma: Poor cat. Poor foot. I'm finding out all sorts of things.

Jess: What like? Is the tennis still good?

Gemma: Tennis is fab 👍 Think my dad might have played.

Jess: wow, that's good

Surinder: UR DAD!!! WOWZERS!!!

Gemma: I've made a few friends too

Surinder: are they as nice as us?

Jess: I hope so! ✌️

Gemma: never! 😁

Chapter Forty

It takes a while to get to Gran's house. We go on roads I haven't been on before and there is lots of traffic.

"Does Gran live where you and Mum grew up?"

"Yep," says Joe. "I'm trying to get her to move but she won't have any of it. Huge great pile for one lady, especially now she's recovering from a broken hip."

We drive down a bumpy lane and then a large pair of wooden gates appear and Joe turns in. A metal sign says *Orchard House*.

"I've never been here," I say.

He glances over. "You have, Gem. But it was a long time ago."

The house has a winding driveway. There are huge, leafy plants either side and then gravel at the top. The scrunch of tyres on the tiny stones reminds me of something but

I can't place it. The house is big, ivy crawling up the walls, red paint peeling on the windowsills. It looks like a house from one of those old TV dramas that Mum watches; crime thrillers and murder mysteries set in the olden days.

Gran opens the front door and steps out on to the gravel, leaning on a frame for support. Crunchy stones again. A memory, familiar and distant.

She has a grey scarf wrapped around her shoulders and she is more hunched over than I've seen her before.

"Darling!" she says and she lifts her hands from the frame and hugs me tight and it feels good. "My lovely Gemma. I hope Joe has been taking good care of you. He can hardly manage to take care of Carrot Cake!"

Joe slams the car boot shut and carries our bags in. "He doesn't deserve looking after. Waste of space."

I laugh. "We had to go back twice this morning, Gran, to check Carrot had water and that the food timer was working properly."

Joe smiles, puts the bags down and helps Gran back into the house. "I was checking I'd locked the door," he says.

"Yeah, right," I say. Two dogs rush out and sniff round our heels.

"The old guy is Copper," says Gran. "You can meet him at last. And that's Tom." She points to the smaller dog with the waggy tail. "The kennels dropped them back this morning." I bend down and stroke them. Copper has to back up to turn round as if he is too stiff to twist.

We go inside. The house is huge and chilly with big rugs on the floor. There is a beautiful stained-glass lamp and an old bike with a basket on the front in the hallway.

We sit round a shiny wooden table in the dining room and eat roast chicken. It's so good with the best roasties and veggies.

"I told you not to do all this, Mum," says Joe.

Gran waves him away. "The carer helped me this morning and it gave me something to do. I hate all this sitting around."

"You're a great cook, Gran," I say, slicing my roast potatoes, the skin crunchy and golden.

"Thanks, love," says Gran. "I bet your mum is too. She used to love baking."

I nod, smile. I've *never* seen Mum bake. "She makes a great stir fry."

"Do you remember that cake she made for my tenth birthday?" says Joe. "The one of the football pitch with all the players and the goalposts?"

I stare at Joe and I'm about to say, "Mum made that?!" but I stop myself. It sounds as if I don't know my own mum. But I've never seen her make a cake. We always buy a caterpillar cake from the supermarket for our birthdays.

Gran nods. "Yes, I remember." She closes her eyes and sighs a little as if it's a bit hard to think about it.

The dining room overlooks the garden. The grass slopes away, rose bushes and small trees dotted down the lawn.

"Anyone want more?" asks Gran.

"Gem will finish the carrots," says Joe. I elbow him gently.

"Would you like more, love?" Gran asks me, and she moves as if to get up, wincing a little. Joe stops her.

"No," says Joe. "It's just a joke between us." Gran sits back and smiles. She looks from one of us to the other and I think she is feeling happy. I think she can tell me and Joe have had a good time.

We eat quietly. Joe tells Gran about his job and I don't understand it much. Gran nods and closes her eyes a bit in a thinking way, as if it helps her to follow what he is saying. We tell her about Mungo having to go back to his owner. Gran's sad about that. She pats my arm and says, "How's your mum getting on?"

"OK, I think. She fell off a donkey."

Gran laughs, really loud.

"I feel sorry for the donkey," says Joe and we all giggle again. He stacks the plates and takes them into the kitchen.

"It's good to laugh!" she says. "How's the tennis camp?"

"Great," I say. "I like it."

"She's a natural apparently!" calls Joe.

Gran smiles at that and wipes her mouth on her serviette. "What's your favourite shot?"

"Forehand, oh, and volleys."

"Sounds great," she says, patting my arm. "We knew you'd love it."

I smile and nod and take a drink. There it is again. The thing everyone has been talking about.

"What's been the hardest bit?" says Gran.

"Scoring. It's so tricky! What game has the word 'deuce' in it?"

Gran laughs at that. "You and Joe ought to watch this year's Wimbledon final. I've still got the men's on record. What d'you think, Joe?" She tries to raise her voice but I think it's an effort to shout. "It would help Gemma to learn the scores."

Joe comes back in, a tea towel tossed over his

shoulder. "Great idea. The ladies' final was brilliant but the men's was an absolute classic! Let's show Gemma how the Spaniard does it!"

And then Gran sighs and winces a little. "Think I need to lie down. I'll leave you to it."

Joe helps her up.

"Be a love, Gem," she says, grabbing on to her walking frame. "Bring me up a glass of water." Joe takes her arm and they head for the stairs, Gran grumbling about the stairlift Joe had insisted on getting. "Makes me feel a hundred!" she says.

I go to the kitchen and find a glass and wait for the water to run cold. From the kitchen window, I can see the garden again, the lawn sloping down to large hedges and bushes. There is a gardener down there, pruning and clipping, a huge bag next to him for the bits he's chopped. I fill the glass. I think I remember how it feels to run down that sloping lawn, how it feels to dodge in and out of the rose bushes and roll on the grass.

The glass overfills, water running down my hands. I turn the tap off and wipe the glass dry and carry it upstairs, passing Joe on the landing. It's a long landing, with doors coming off on each side.

"Her room's there, on the right," he says.

I go into Gran's room and put the drink down on the bedside table.

"Here you go," I say, but when I look across, she is asleep. I pull the blanket round her and move the glass further away so it can't be knocked.

The bedside table is dusty. There are little stripes, as if things have been removed, leaving clear telltale lines behind. They're just like the ones Mum and I uncovered when we dusted at home. I wonder if the elephant is gathering dust again, little specks settling in the grooves of its trunk. It seems funny to think about all those tiny things happening in our empty flat while we are away.

At the back of the table are photos in frames. One of Gran and Grandpa on the beach when they were young, eating fish and chips out of newspaper wrappers. Grandpa is pulling a piece of fish free but Gran is looking straight at the camera, her eyes bright and full of joy. There is a smaller photo, of Joe and Mum when they were children. I lift it up, turn it over, read on the back *Carrie and Joe, aged four and two*. I put the frame on the table, matching it exactly to its dust-free stripe. There is one other photo but on the wall, just behind the bedside table in a large silver frame. It's the same photo that Joe has on the landing of his house. Me and Mum on Joe's wedding day. That tight line of Mum's mouth, the tilt of her head, her right hand twisting her silver hoops and me, small and shy, holding my posy of flowers.

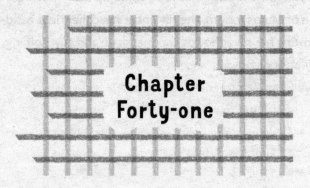

Chapter Forty-one

Joe is arguing with the TV. "How many controls can one person *have*?" he says, pressing endless buttons.

I sit on the sofa and look at the paintings on the wall, at the old chairs and rugs and the two dogs lying by the patio doors. I'm wearing my shorts and the sofa is scratchy on my legs. I imagine Mum being here in this grand old house, growing up, running down that huge lawn.

Everything about our life is so small and cramped and simple. I think about our tiny flat with the welcome sign on the door and I ache to be home. Ache to sit on our stained old sofa that Mum has covered in blankets, watch our silly old TV that sometimes goes blurred and dies, sit at our kitchen table with the two red chairs that have *Gem's* and *Mum's* painted on the back with gold nail varnish.

And then I hear the thud of tennis balls and the grunt of someone hitting them hard and the cheers of a huge crowd.

"I'll forward to the last set," says Joe, pointing the control at the screen. "It's a long one."

He sits next to me on the sofa.

"I'll take you one day, Gem," he says. "Best place on the planet, Wimbledon Centre Court."

"How many times have you been?"

"A few. And once for the ladies' final. Chris got tickets. He loved tennis. He loved any sport." Joe pulls his hands through his hair. "He loved life."

The balls are smacked so hard. It's fun to watch the speed, the power. I get the giggles.

"What?" says Joe. "What's so funny?"

"Just thinking about me and Flori. Not quite the same, is it?!"

Joe talks me through every shot. He explains the dominance of the service, how the server normally wins the game, how the return of serve is so important. The Swiss player has an amazing return. Joe shows me how he takes the ball so early, so fast.

The game flies by. Joe gets a tin from the kitchen, pops open the lid and we wade through Gran's biscuits.

Tom nuzzles at our feet, picking up crumbs, loping off once the carpet is clean.

The Spaniard is fast and fiercely strong.

"But you see," says Joe, "he has amazing touch too. Look! Look! Right there. Two points from victory and look at the touch. Look at that lob just gliding overhead. No way that can be chased down." He sits back and marvels at the replay. "That was your mum's *best* shot. She could lob anyone. She would hoist it and put so much topspin on it that it would fly off the back—" He stops.

I freeze. His words rifle through me, carry through my blood to my fingertips, to the end of my tongue, like it sets something fizzing through me. My breath is deep and heavy, juddering in my mouth as I let it out. We both sit, incredibly still in the quiet of the moment.

The Spaniard serves for the set, for the championship. Aces the serve, the crowd erupts and Joe and I just sit, staring at the screen. We sit while the Spaniard climbs up the Wimbledon steps and hugs his family. We sit while the loser is shown, head bent, hidden by his towel. We sit as the preparations are made for the trophy to be given out, as the ballgirls and boys line up on the court and then with a sudden crack, the recording stops.

Silence.

Copper gets up and looks around, pads out to the kitchen for a drink. Joe picks up the remote and switches the TV off.

"We didn't see him get his trophy," I say. I am still frozen, staring at the screen.

"No," says Joe, laying the remotes in a straight line. "We didn't."

Thoughts flood in, spill round. I stand up and head for the stairs.

"Gemma," says Joe. "Wait..." But I know where answers are.

The landing is quiet. I open Gran's door but I've chosen the wrong room. It is a bathroom, a pink bathroom, with ruffly curtains.

I try the next door. Gran is asleep, her soft hair resting on the pillow. I sit on the bed and her eyes open.

"Hey, Gem," she says. "Are you OK?"

"Sort of," I say. I stare at the bedside table. "You didn't drink your water."

"Now," she says. "Now would be good."

I pass her the glass and she groans as she lifts herself up. And then I run my fingers along the stripes on the bedside table, mix in the dust to make squiggly lines.

"Where are they?" I say. "I know, Gran, about Mum. Joe just told me. He didn't mean to. Where are the pictures?" She takes a sip and stares at me, hands me the glass and leans back, wincing a little.

"You have no idea how much we all love you," she says, patting my leg.

"I need to know," I say.

She looks at me for a moment, closes her eyes and then nods to the drawer in the bedside table. "In there," she says. "I shouldn't have hidden them. I just panicked a bit, that's all. Your mum didn't want you to find out. We all knew that."

I pull the handle and the drawer slides open and there, in a pile, are four framed photos with some of the answers I have been looking for.

Chapter Forty-two

Joe comes in and sits in the armchair beside the bed. He kicks his long legs out and runs his hands through his fringe, his eyes resting on us.

The first photo is him and Mum as teenagers. Mum has braces and her hair is in bunches, two bananas of hair sticking out from her head. They are standing arm in arm, their rackets crossed, big smiles beaming at the camera. I wipe the dust off the top and place it back on the bedside table. The second is just Mum, a few years older, a more serious look on her face. She is holding a gold trophy. The third is Gran, Grandpa, Joe and Mum, all in tennis kit, standing on a court with a large bush behind them. Joe's hair is short, almost shaved short, and he is skinny. They have just thrown balls into the air, their arms held high. Just Gran's ball is still in the picture, framed by blue sky as it flies up.

The last frame contains a newspaper article. It is Mum at the airport, standing by two huge holdalls, rackets sticking out of one of them. She is waving a large flag with stars on it and the headline says *SUPERSTAR TENNIS CHAMP HEADS TO USA TO TRAIN*.

I stare at the photo. Tennis has nothing to do with my dad. It is *my mum*. She was the player. She is the talent, the blood.

I know less about my dad than ever.

"She didn't want you to know about the tennis, Gem," says Gran.

"But why?" I ask.

I look up at Gran and Joe. They are staring at each other, not sure what to say.

"It's complicated," says Joe.

I nod a little. There is so much to ask but I'm not sure where to start. I look back at the photo, the one of the four of them tossing balls into the air. The camera is held at a funny angle. You can just see their faces and upheld hands. Behind the hedge, there is a house, a big, brick house with red windowsills and white and purple flowers.

Joe's right. I *have* been here before.

I stand up and walk out of the room.

Joe calls to me but I am running by then, taking the stairs two at a time, flying through the kitchen, out towards the back door. The dogs get to their feet, joining in with the excitement.

The lawn is damp and sloping and I dodge in and out of the rose bushes, just as I did when I was five years old, back from the wedding, the nightmare of the horrid bride with her white train done with. I glance back and see the purple flowers all along the back of the house, climbing round the door. The memories flood in, each bumping into the next.

The gardener's bag of cuttings is there but he has gone. I run alongside the hedge, the tall green hedge, searching for the gap. And there it is, the small wooden gate.

I am five again, about the height of the gate, excited to discover this hidden world. The moment tips back into my mind, slowly at first and then gathering pace until the memories flood in, spilling and rolling over each other. Mum is pulling on my ribbons and bridesmaid dress, urging me with a desperate tug to leave the gate, dragging me back up the lawn to have my photo taken with her.

They want one of me and you, she had said, my

hand clenched in hers, bribing me with the most amazing treats of ice cream and toys and gifts. All those things, if I would just stand still and smile for the camera and forget about the gate.

Leave the gate and on the way home we'll stop and buy that doll you want.

I wanted that doll so much. So I left the gate and stood and smiled and she had held on to me and smiled that painful smile that was to be framed and hung on walls.

―――――――――

On the journey home, she had told the taxi driver to drive to the nearest giant toy store. The shop assistant was locking up, a bunch of keys rattling in his hand.

"Sorry, love, we're closing."

She had pleaded with him, one tear running down her face.

"Vital," she had sobbed. "This is vital." She had pointed at me, standing there in my pink dress with chocolate sauce and grass stains down the front. "Please. I made a promise."

He had nodded as if he understood and we had run

up and down the aisles until we found the shiny rubber doll in the plastic box, the one with the long lashes and eyes that flicked open and shut.

It's strange but I have always remembered buying that doll, Mum's face pleading with the man, running up and down the aisles, Mum tipping out her purse to find the money, the use of the word "vital" that I had never heard before. But it is only now, standing by this gate, that I remember we had bought it after the wedding and that I had still been wearing my pink dress.

We had driven home in the taxi in silence, me tucked next to Mum, holding the doll of my dreams. Mum had wiped her tears away, one by one, until she gave up and let them roll quite freely down her cheeks, the drips falling on to her lap. I can see those tears now, so clearly, falling one by one. And I can remember tipping the doll up and down, very gently, to see if tears came out of her eyes.

Chapter
Forty-three

I tug and wrench the gate, yank it hard until it gives way, the bottom dragging on the undergrowth. It opens straight on to the court. I walk in, scrape my shoe on the moss that covers the lines, reach the net that sags and dips, the middle section torn and ripped. And then I turn round and I think of the photo. I am standing in the very spot where the four of them had stood, throwing balls into the air, the hedge and the house rising up behind them.

There is a ball in the corner. I walk over and pick it up. A spider's web pulls from it, breaks in two before I have a chance to realize.

"Sorry," I whisper to the spider.

I bounce the ball on the ground. It has no bounce left, just rolls a short distance and stops.

The gate squeaks. Joe comes in.

"You OK?" he says.

I nod.

"I'm sorry, Gem, that you found out about your mum this way." He puts his hands in his pockets, stares at the ground, looks back at me.

"Why did she never tell me?" I say. "I don't get it. Why's it all been kept from me?"

He blinks hard, tries to find the right words but nothing comes out.

And then I get it. "The fallout. It's linked to all this, isn't it? That's why she never said anything, why I never knew."

He looks at me slowly, nods his head. "I feel so bad it's all come out now, while you're with me. I shouldn't have enrolled you in the tennis camp but the timing of it worked so brilliantly with you coming to stay and I hoped you had played a bit. I didn't stop to think about all the questions it might lead to." His voice breaks, he gulps a little. "I was so angry with her for so many years and I shouldn't have been." He wraps his arm around me. There are biscuit crumbs down his jumper. I brush them off, lean into him.

"For having me?" I mumble. "You were angry at her for having me?"

He whips round and grabs my shoulders, his hands firmly on me, stands back and bends low to look right into my eyes.

"No, never. We loved you from the *very* start, you must believe that?" His eyes are wide and pleading. "We loved you so much. But it was hard. Your mum refused to *ever* play tennis again. She said she hadn't really wanted to go to America, that she had had enough anyway, that she wanted to go to college and just enjoy being a mum. But we wouldn't believe her … didn't listen to her."

He stops for a moment. I run my hands along the net, pick at the holes. He takes a deep breath, carries on. "Once we knew the score, we should have backed off, let her live her life the way she wanted to. But we didn't."

I laugh gently, look up at him.

"What?" says Joe.

"It's just that 'knowing the score' thing," I say. "Like in tennis, it's so tricky."

He smiles. "Yes, everything is easier when you know the score. In life and in tennis!"

I scuff my shoe on the mossy ground. "So what happened, when you didn't back off?"

Joe sighs, looks up at the sky.

"You were about six months old and we all piled the

pressure on her to start playing again. Dad was ill and he was desperate for Carrie to fulfill her potential. She had won a massive tournament before she went to America. Coaches were contacting us all the time."

"Wow," I say, "I can't imagine it."

"Gran was frustrated. I didn't help," says Joe. "I was seventeen. I felt angry, cheated. I wanted her talent. I would have done *anything* to have her talent."

"You were jealous of her?" I say, squinting at him in the sunshine, trying to make sense of it all.

"*So* jealous. I took it out on her, said some dreadful things. And then one day ... one day I did it in front of you." He stops, panics a little, puts one hand up as if to defend himself. "I didn't *know* you were there. I thought you were out with Gran. But you were asleep in your stroller in the hall." He stops, looks down, rubs his face. When he looks up again, there is a tear running down his cheek. "I had asked her to play with me, to help me practise, enter a doubles tournament I was keen to play in. But she refused. So I yelled, called her something terrible and the shock of the noise woke you up, made you cry. I think that was the tipping point and I don't blame her at all. She lifted you out of the stroller and told me that if I couldn't accept her decision, then she

229

would never speak to me again." He waits, catches his breath, looks up at the trees.

I watch Joe for a moment, try to think, to understand. "Did she?" I say. "Did she speak to you again?"

"I thought she would. I just thought it was the heat of the moment. But she meant it. After that we hardly spoke for years, not until the wedding, when we tried to make things better."

"Mmm," I say and I nod. There is so much to take in. "So the two of you fell out but she stayed here at first, at the house?"

"Yes, that was really tricky. Gran hated the fact we weren't speaking. And then Dad became very poorly." He stops for a second, sniffs deeply. "He was dying and he selfishly made it his dying wish to see Carrie play again. Gran spent a lot of time caring for him, but she still tried to get Carrie back on the court, tried persuading her to juggle both things, tennis and you, use childcare, but Carrie wouldn't even talk about it. It made things almost impossible. So much time and money and investment had gone into her tennis. She could have been an international player, had a full career. It was tough for them to watch her throw it away."

"For me." I am crying now, the tears flowing freely. "She threw it all away for me."

Joe hugs me and I sob. "No, not for you, Gem. She gave it up because she didn't *want* it any more."

We stand for a while like that and then he pulls back. "She didn't want to play tennis any more but we wouldn't listen to her. Wouldn't understand. We gave her a hard time. And we paid for it. She left home, backed away, wouldn't have much to do with us at all. Only let Gran see you a few times a year and never here at the house. She wanted to protect you ... refused to even *talk* about tennis. Ever. Wouldn't return my calls. I don't blame her at all, not now. Not after the way I behaved, the way we all did. She didn't want that in your life, or hers."

We wander round the court a little, stop in the shade of one of the giant trees.

"That must be why she never told me anything," I say. "About it all."

"Yes," says Joe. "We made life unbearable for her. And we wouldn't back down. I think she had to start over, with you. We always thought she would come back, *need* to come back, but *boy*..." he stops, looks up at the sky, throws his head back down, "is she one *headstrong* cookie!"

231

I smile and nod. We walk on. "I can't imagine you being angry."

He stops and looks around the court, swipes fallen leaves with his foot. "Not now, no, Gem. But I was then. I was seventeen and super jealous."

"Can I ask one more thing?" I say.

"Of course," says Joe. "Anything."

"The wedding. Why didn't the fresh start work?"

He smiles, shakes his head. "You know what, Gem? I don't really know. We started planning it and she came over to the house, let you have dress fittings. I'd learned my lesson by then, I had apologized and grown up. We tried to make it better, tried to show we loved you both very much but I'm not sure any of us were really ready."

"I don't think I helped." I can feel the tears brewing again. I fight them back.

"You were amazing! Why do you say that?"

I bite my lip, try so hard not to cry. "At the wedding, I found that gate." We both turn to look at it. "I remember now, quite clearly. I wanted to see what was behind it. She tried to get me away, promised me if I would just have my photo taken we would leave then and she'd buy me a new doll I really wanted."

Joe stares at me for a moment and slowly nods,

as if pieces of that day are falling into place for him too. "That's why she left so quickly..."

"Yep."

"Well, that explains things but none of it matters now."

We walk on, the sunshine warming our faces. A bird flies very low, right over the court. We are so quiet that we hear its wings, the air against its body. We both follow its path, up into the trees.

"They always used to fly low like that," he says, smiling. "I haven't been on this court for years, probably since the days I played with your mum."

"Was she really good?" I ask, pulling crumpled leaves off the black grids of the nylon net.

He looks down at me and waits for a second and then he says, "Awesome. She was awesome."

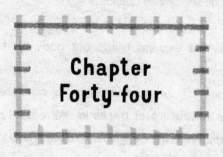

Chapter
Forty-four

We play cards that night, lots of card games I've never heard of. Newmarket, rummy, cheat. No one talks about tennis. We just play cards and it's fun.

Mum messages Joe to say she's off the boat with a weak signal and is it OK if we speak tomorrow. I'm a little relieved. I'm exhausted and my head is spinning, trying to understand it all. We message back to say it's fine and send loads of love. From all of us.

It's late when we go to bed. I wash in the pink bathroom where Gran had dressed me for the wedding. The same ruffly curtains hang at the window. I run my fingers through the pleats, just as I had done that day.

My room has a huge bed covered in a patchwork quilt.

"One of my hobbies," says Gran when she comes to say goodnight, pushing her frame up to the bed. "Patchworking, making the pieces all make sense. Like a puzzle." She turns back the sheets and plumps the pillow. "Hope you sleep well. It's been a good day, tough but good. I think your mum will be relieved, Gem, that you know the truth."

"I hope so, Gran. I'm glad I know." She kisses me and leaves.

There are shelves of books in the room. Fairy tales, classics and old books with leather covers. They make me think of Flori. I flick through them and pull out one called *Open*. A man's face stares at me from the cover. There is a knock on the door.

"Come in," I call. It's Joe with Copper at his feet.

"Great book," he says, tapping the cover. "It's Agassi's story. Andre Agassi, best returner ever in my opinion, fighter extraordinaire."

He takes the book and opens the front page and shows me the message written in red, swirly letters. *Best man, best mate. Thanks for always being there. Chris.*

"Chris gave it to me the day he married Sophie."

He passes me back the book.

"You should take it home with you," I say.

"Yes, I will," says Joe. "Gran borrowed it and it just ended up staying here." He looks out of the window into the dark night. "It seemed to belong here, really."

Copper waddles over and sniffs at his hand. Joe strokes his head. "Come on, Copper, old boy." He pulls the curtain across. "Sleep tight, Gem."

I nod and smile and he leaves with Copper padding behind, a twig hanging out of his tail.

The bed is snuggly and cosy, the sheets as soft as felt. I stare at the rows and rows of books, at the wooden-framed windows, the moonlight glinting into the room. Was this Mum's room? Did she sleep here the night before she left for America?

I turn over and then back again, pulling the covers around me. Everything is different now. Every memory that pops up has a newness about it. Like it's been painted in a different colour.

Mum and Gran and Joe. I understand now. I know the truth. But I have so many questions, hundreds of them, spilling round, bumping into each other. My mum, completely on her own for all those years. My dad, in America. Joe and Gran left sad and upset.

I sit up, hug my knees and for some strange reason, I think of when I helped Sophie to fill the big jar of cat biscuits. It was hard at first, to get the biscuits out of the bag. The hole was too small, the biscuits got caught in the rim. We had to tip it at a different angle, make the hole slightly bigger. And then the biscuits dislodged themselves, broke free and gathered pace until they flooded out, filling the jar and then spilling over on to the counter. We had swept them up with a cloth, Bobby nibbling beside us on the ones he could reach.

That's how things feel right now. Like Joe cut the corner of the past and let everything flow out. Thoughts and memories filter through slowly, get stuck and then flow fast, out of control, spilling over. I'd like to sweep them up and put them in a tin, just like we did with the biscuits. Put the lid on tight, shake it hard and let them all settle into one even pile, ordered and sorted.

I lie back, take a deep breath.

I know why the fallout happened, I know the truth about Mum.

The truth is so much better.

Much better than not knowing.

Now I need to find a way to fix it, mend things, get the family back on track. I have to. I can't imagine not spending more time with Joe and Gran, especially here at Orchard House.

It's Mum I've got to convince and I'm worried she might not feel the same.

> **Surinder:** The pool was closed today. Some kid did a number two in it.

> **Jess:** aww nooooo poor kid!!!!

> **Gemma:** I'm at Gran's with her dogs. She has two.

> **Jess:** what are their names?

> **Gemma:** Tom and Copper

> **Jess:** 👍

I start to write a message. *And guess what? My mum was this superstar tennis player and my dad's probably in America.* But something stops me sending it. I need to speak to Mum first. It's not right to share yet. I press delete and the message disappears and instead I write:

> **Gemma:** I'm in the biggest cosiest bed you have ever seen.

Jess: soooo cool Gem

Surinder: I'm lying on a stinky rubber blow up bed and the wind is rattling the tent and the guy next door is snoring soooo loud you can hear it 😠

Jess: 😞 ⛺

Chapter
Forty-five

We all sleep in late. Joe makes bacon sandwiches and then we walk the dogs. It's raining so I borrow Gran's big, oily coat with giant pockets. The pockets are stuffed with poo bags and hankies, pebbles and mint sweets. I zip the coat up and nestle into it. It smells of her: cooking and perfume, old blankets and dogs. We cross the river and stop on a bench for the dogs to have a rest. Joe's phone rings.

"It's your mum," he says. "Shall I answer?"

I nod. He passes me the phone.

"Hi," I say. I get off the bench and walk over to a clump of bracken on the side of the path, tapping it and hooking my foot through the brambles. Tom joins me, panting and sniffing at the ground.

"Hi, darling, how are you?"

"Fine."

I don't know what to say. How do I start? The calm I felt when I woke up has gone. I'm irritated now, about all the things I never knew.

"What you doing?" she says in her sing-song voice that she uses when she desperately wants everything to be OK but she knows it's not.

"Just walking the dogs," I say. "Although dragging the dogs is more like it."

She laughs at that. "Copper's the same age as you. He'll be feeling it now. How's Gran?"

"Tired, but fine. We played cards last night. She won most of the games."

"She's canny," says Mum. We are quiet for a moment. Copper walks over and rests at my feet. "Gem..."

"I know, Mum. I know everything. I know you were an amazing tennis player. I know about you going to America to play and then having me and then never playing tennis again."

I bend down to stroke Copper and fight the strong need to cry.

"Thought you might," says Mum. "Couldn't see how you could go to Orchard House and not. I'm sorry, Gemma. I'm sorry I never told you what happened.

I had planned to when you were older and then the years just flew by. It never seemed the right time and I suppose, deep down, I didn't want you to know."

I can feel Joe watching me and I can feel Mum's worry down the line.

"It feels like I ruined everything," I say.

Mum gasps a little, like you do when something on TV makes you jump.

"Oh, Gem," she says. "No!" And then she is quiet and so am I. There is just the sound of the raindrops on the trees and Tom nuzzling in the ferns and the faint crackling of the forest undergrowth.

"Right," says Mum. "Listen carefully." She speaks very slowly and firmly as if it is important I hear every word. "Having you *made* my life." She gulps hard, trying not to cry. "You are the most important thing to me, *ever.*"

I wonder how much this call is costing, this call linking a drizzling forest in the countryside with the Caribbean cruise ship.

"This isn't the time to talk about all of this," she says. "But I want you to know one thing. I'd already had enough of tennis before you came along. I wanted to stop, go to college, but it all just seemed impossible, like I was on this unstoppable journey. You came along and I knew for sure what I wanted. If I'd wanted to play, Gem, I *could* have carried on. Gran found me a nanny to look after you. But *I* wanted to look after you. I had all the support in the world but I didn't want to play tennis. I had you and you were all I needed, all I wanted."

Copper sits beside me, leans his head against my leg.

"I am pretty special," I say, smiling.

"Just a bit," says Mum. "When I get home, we will talk about all of this. I'll tell you everything. Anything you want to know."

A couple walk past with their dog on a lead, smiling at me like I am having a perfectly normal conversation about homework or a sleepover or picking up pizza on the way home.

"Are you OK?" says Mum.

"I'm fine."

"Gem, I can't hear you very well, the line's not great."

"I want to know about my dad."

The line is quiet. For a moment I think the signal is lost. But then Mum says, "We can talk about that too."

And then the phone beeps as if the signal is truly lost.

"Mum," I say. "Can you hear me?" But the line has gone. I tap the screen as if that will help but the call is over. And now I feel bad. All I need is my mum. I need her to know that.

I shove the phone in my pocket, walk through the bracken, into the forest, the branches flicking on my cheek. I bury myself deep in a patch of trees and slump down on the ground, the wet leaves quickly soaking through my shorts. I want to tell Mum I love her. I get the phone out again but there is no signal. None at all. There is just a scratch right across the screen where the phone has rubbed against the stones in Gran's pocket.

Joe and I finish the walk in silence. My cheek is bleeding from one of the snappy branches. I dig in Gran's pocket for a hanky. I find one and I pass Joe his phone.

"I'm sorry, Joe, look..." I say as I press the hanky to my face.

He puts his arm around me. "It really doesn't matter, Gem," he says. "Nothing survives Gran's pockets."

We walk on, Joe guiding me back to the house, Copper and Tom loping alongside. I wonder about asking Joe if I can call Mum back. But he has to stop and clear up after the dogs and then Sophie calls and it no longer feels the right time.

When we get back, Gran asks Joe to make a fire. "I love a summer fire," she says. "Just a bit of warmth." The patio doors are open, fresh air drifting in, the rain falling steadily on the lawn. The dogs are stretched out on the rug.

"Mum and I talked," I say to Gran. "I think she was a bit upset."

"She will be," says Gran, stroking Copper's head. "But probably also a little relieved, Gem, that the truth is out. It will take time. But hopefully this is the start of a new beginning. Of us all being together again."

"I hope so." Being together again sounds so good. I'm just worried Mum might not want that.

We sit and watch the fire and then Gran gets out a box of chocolates and a pack of cards and we play again. Joe teaches me this game where two players face each other and lay out their cards in a certain order and then bang, you're off and it's fast and somehow turning over the Queen and the Jack and making the twos all fit in a pile helps. Like the slapping of the cards slaps away a tiny bit of the worry.

Chapter
Forty-six

We have tea and get ready to leave. Gran is tired but I can tell she's happy. Her carer arrives to help her.

I nestle into Tom and Copper. "I'll see you boys soon," I tell them and I give Gran a big hug.

We drive home with the music really loud and the sun golden in the sky. We both know the words to one song and we sing it out, Joe tapping the steering wheel and me using my water bottle like a microphone. It's such fun Joe plays it again and we sing even louder.

Carrot Cake is waiting on the front step when we get home.

"Look at him," says Joe. "Honestly. Like he's put out we left him."

"Well, I'm thrilled to see him." I undo my seat belt and get out and scoop him up. He sinks into my arms, his paws either side of my neck.

"Absolute waste of space," says Joe, putting his key in the door and giving him a tickle under the chin. "First job, laundry, Gem. Get all your kit and we'll give it a wash, ready for tomorrow." I nod and run upstairs and come down with my bag of washing. There are two machines in the utility room.

"Which one do I use?" I ask. Joe points to the left one. It seems so easy, just doing the laundry at home. I think of me and Mum, taking the bags to the launderette and then lugging them back up the hill.

Joe adds a few things of his to the drum. One of the tops has a Velcro collar and a pink sock is stuck to it.

"Is this yours?" he asks, showing me.

"Um, no," I say. "I think it must be Lexi's."

"Oh," he says. He folds the sock and leaves it on the worktop.

I stare at the numbers and dials. "Will you see her later to give it back?"

Joe presses a button and the machine jumps into life. "No, I won't be seeing her for a while, Gem."

"Oh," I say.

"We're taking a break. It's been on the cards for some time."

I nod. "I hope it's not me being here."

Joe smiles. "My lovely niece, it has absolutely nothing to do with you being here. Although I do wonder if you've shown me a few things, Gemma, about life and stuff." He laughs, opens his eyes wide as if saying those words surprised him a little. "We just don't quite work, me and Lexi."

I don't know what to say to that. And then I think about Minxie and him laughing about the duel, the way she'd plugged her phone in Joe's car like she'd done it a hundred times before, phoning him when Lexi had gone to the gym.

"You won't see Minxie much now, will you?" It's strange how sorry I feel for her.

"No," says Joe, moving the pink sock away, along the counter, out of sight. "And that's a shame."

Carrot Cake jumps up on to the worktop.

"I want to show you something," says Joe. He lifts Carrot down and I follow him into the kitchen.

There is a photo album on the island. I sit on the stool and place my hands on the cool stainless steel. Joe leans on the counter beside me. He opens the first page.

"I made this album when you were born. Your mum was so incredibly in love with you. We all were." He points to the first page. "We still are."

He watches as I look at each page. It's so odd seeing all these new photos. Mum has a few of me as a baby in a frame next to her bed, but those are the only ones I've seen. We don't have an album like this.

There are lots of photos. Gran, Grandpa, Uncle Joe. All eleven years younger. Mum's hair is longer, flowing down her back, sometimes up in a ponytail. I'm held high, giggling. I'm lying on the lawn with Gran, Orchard House in the background. I'm with Joe on a swing, my chubby hands in his. I turn each page, soaking up the details of my early life. One of me in a little baby chair and then propped up with cushions. There is a lady with me I don't know, maybe the nanny Mum had mentioned. Copper is there, a cute puppy, playing with a tennis ball.

"Everyone looks so happy here," I say. "Like there are no problems at all."

"There weren't at first," says Joe. "We just thought your mum would need a bit of time and then she'd be back playing again." He stares at the photos, rubs a hand fondly over one of his mum and dad. "That was just a few weeks before he died." He stops, sighs. "It seems so ridiculous now, looking back, that we even cared about the tennis." He sniffs a bit, blinks. "I just felt so frustrated with your mum. That was wrong of me. It's no wonder she struck me out of her life." I watch Joe for a second and I feel this massive love for my mum. It must have been so hard for her.

I turn the pages and we both look, not saying anything, letting the photos fill the air until they run out. I don't want them to run out. I want to keep turning, keep watching my life when I was little.

The last photo is me and Mum on the beach. She is carrying me on her hip, walking down to the sea, a bucket and spade in her right hand. Then there are a few empty back pages. I flick back to the start again, looking at each page.

Joe gets up and puts the kettle on. "I'll be back in a mo," he says. I nod and he goes upstairs.

Each page tells so much. And yet so much was going on that the photos don't tell. The discussions about Mum's life, her tennis, arguments about her getting back on the court. None of that is there. I turn the empty pages at the back. They are stuck together so I peel them apart, hoping to find a few more photos. There aren't any but I find something else instead. A newspaper cutting, different to the one Gran had in the frame, from a year or so before. This one shows Mum, age sixteen, standing in a row of five players, each with their rackets, the headline above their heads: *National Under 17 Squad Head to France*.

Joe comes back in and reaches for two mugs. "Hot chocolate?" he says.

"Yes, please," I say. I read the article, turn it over to see if there is anything on the back, peel the other pages in the album to see if there are any more cuttings.

"What's that you've found?" asks Joe, putting my mug in front of me. I hold up the article. He takes it, tilts his head, reads it. "Wow, I didn't realize that was in there."

"The national team?" I ask. "The *national* team?"

Joe smiles. "Yep, she was that good." I put it back, close the album, push it away. Joe sits down again next to me. "But she didn't want it any more, Gem. It's super tough being at the top of any sport. You have to want it with all your heart."

I reach for my mug, wrap my hands around it.

"I think," he says, "if I'd had that much talent, I would have wanted it with *all* my heart. I blamed her for not feeling the same."

We both sip our drinks.

"Thanks for showing me the photos," I say. "I love them."

"They mean a lot to me," he says. Carrot Cake jumps

up next to us and snuggles into Joe. "Much more than this waste of space." But he picks him up and tickles him under his chin and I stroke his head over and over and I think about Mungo and how he might be getting on.

Joe goes to check on the laundry and I turn the pages again, look at Mum's face; happy and relaxed, full of love. And then the photos stop and I think of the tough years Mum must have faced and how she became so alone. Just me and her. On our own. How hard it must have been for her.

I'm not sure I want to go to tennis camp tomorrow.

I'm not sure about anything any more.

Chapter
Forty-seven

"She doesn't want to play," says Joe. He is on his mobile, pacing up and down the hallway, jangling his keys in one hand. "I'm not sure what to do, Soph. Monday is a hard day for me not to be in the office. I don't understand why she suddenly doesn't..."

I come out of the kitchen, carrying my bowl of cereal.

"I'll just stay here," I say.

"Not an option," says Joe, shaking his head at me. "Not all day."

Carrot Cake winds himself round my legs. I rub him on the tummy with my mules. I am back in my mules and they feel good. I've cut little holes in the end to make more space for my toes.

Joe is nodding and talking in a low voice and then he hangs up.

"I'm a problem, aren't I?" I say.

Joe smiles. "No," he says. "You're not. Sophie's going to spend the morning with you. She can juggle things. We'll meet her at the club."

We are in the car when Mum rings. All the calls in Joe's car come through the speaker but he presses a button and tells me to pick up his phone and it's just me and Mum.

"I'm going to come home early, Gem," she says.

I'm not expecting her to say that. I'm missing her but it makes me feel strange, thinking of Mum cutting her wonderful trip short, me not spending more time with Joe.

"No, Mum, you really don't need to."

"I think I do. I want you to hear the truth from me, not from everyone there. We pull into port tonight and I'm going to see if I can leave the boat and fly home."

"I don't want you to," I say. "I really don't. It's not long now. Just enjoy the sunshine."

There is a silence between us. I don't want to go home early. I want to be with Joe a bit longer. It's raining a little and I watch the drizzle on the windscreen, follow the trail of raindrops.

"There's nothing else I need to know," I say. "Not

right now. We can talk about the rest when you're back. And about my dad."

Joe shifts in his seat and glances at me.

Mum is quiet.

"Mum? Are you there? I'm not playing tennis today." I'm hoping that might make her happy.

"Why?" she says, very quickly. "It's great that you're playing. I've been thinking about it a lot. As frustrated as I am with that brother of mine, it sounds like you're enjoying it and that's good."

"Too late now," I say. "I'm spending the day with Sophie."

We pull into the tennis club. Sophie's car is parked up. Bradley is on the court already, hitting the ball high into the air, him and Raj looking up, waiting for it to drop. It seems odd that I'm not joining them. I slump down in my seat, glad that the drizzle is hiding me a little. I want to leave quickly, before they all notice.

Joe turns the engine off.

"Mum, are you there?"

"Yes, I am. Did you hear what I said?"

"Yes, I did. I've got to go. Sophie's here."

"I thought..." she says. "I thought you would want me to come home."

"I do. But not yet." Joe looks at me and gives me a little smile. "Bye, Mum. Let's talk later. I love you."

"OK. Bye, Gem, love you," says Mum and she hangs up.

We sit quietly for a moment.

Sophie comes out of the clubhouse. She waves at me and comes round to my side and opens the door and leans in.

"Come on, lovely girl," she says, taking my hand. "Let's go for a smoothie. You've saved me from a really boring finance meeting. Thank you!"

"OK, Gem?" says Joe and I nod and climb into Sophie's car and she drives off straight away and I'm so glad.

Chapter
Forty-eight

We drive for a bit and pull up at a little row of shops. Smoothie Paradise has stools at the window and fake flowers round the door.

We go in and look at a big board with all the smoothie options. I choose vanilla and strawberry. It comes with a little umbrella on top.

"Please let me pay," I say, getting my ten-pound note out of my pocket.

"No way," says Sophie.

We sit on green stools looking out over the road.

"My mum would like this place," I say.

"She has good taste," says Sophie.

I smile at that and stir my smoothie, mixing in the little flecks of strawberry.

"Have you heard anything about Mungo?" I ask.

"No," says Sophie. "I'll call them soon to check he's OK. We might be getting some kittens. They were found yesterday, abandoned."

I whip round and look at her. "Why would anyone abandon kittens?"

Sophie shrugs and leans towards me a little. "I have *no* idea, Gem, no idea at all."

We slurp on our drinks. It's still raining and the windows are a little steamy. I run my finger down the glass, making a line in the steam.

"So," says Sophie. "Joe told me about the weekend and everything coming out."

I put on my best ghost voice. "Dun dun dun ... everything coming out..."

Sophie stares at me for a few seconds. "You found out your mum was a tennis superstar."

I nod and stir, take out the little umbrella and open and close it.

"Why didn't you want to play today?" she asks.

I just shrug.

"Did you know?" I say, wiping my straw round the glass. "Did you know about my mum?"

"Yes," says Sophie. "I knew."

I pick at the wooden struts of the little umbrella,

peel the paper away from them and put them in a pile. "Everyone knew except me."

"That's tough," says Sophie. "But I'm sure your mum had her reasons."

I stare at my drink.

"And I'm sure your mum wouldn't want you to worry about it."

I wait for a moment, watch the cars drive by. "She told me she didn't want to keep playing anyway, that she'd had enough and was ready to give it up and go to college. And then when I was born, she just wanted to take care of me." Sophie nods, waits for me to carry on. So I do. I tell her everything. Everything I know, all the stuff I found out over the weekend about tennis and the family fallout and Joe.

"It's a lot for you to take in," says Sophie.

"Yes," I say.

"It feels a little bit to me..." says Sophie. She stops and looks up and thinks carefully before she carries on. "It's a little bit like all these things have been tucked away for so long, like things in a cupboard, and the doors were only just kept shut and now it's all spilling out. And soon it will all be folded a bit more neatly so it can be sorted through and stored a little more easily."

I think about that. It's good. I smile and say, "Yes, that's very much how it feels."

"The lovely thing, Gemma, is that everything you need is in that cupboard. It just needs a good tidy up."

"And," I say, "a wash and an iron."

Sophie smiles. We finish our smoothies in silence. Sophie sees someone she knows but she just raises her hand, doesn't go over to talk.

"It's not right that I play tennis," I say.

"I don't think that's true."

"It didn't make Mum happy. So I don't think I should play. I just want to stay at home." That makes me think of Mum and our home and a wave of homesickness floods through me. I slurp the last of my smoothie, try to take my mind off it.

"I can understand that," says Sophie. "Some days life can feel very tricky. I have days like that. Sometimes I miss Chris so badly that I just want to snuggle under the blankets and let the hours pass. But that doesn't help anyone, especially Bradley."

I wipe my finger round the rim of my glass. "Or cats like Mungo."

"Or cats like lovely Mungo," she says, nodding.

We both stare out at the street, watch the cars as

they pass by, the puddles spraying off the tyres.

"I'm not sure you *not* playing solves anything," she says. "Do you like it?"

"What?"

"Playing tennis. Do you like it?"

I stare at the road and nod.

Sophie sighs. "You know, I'm not sure *your* tennis and your mum's tennis have anything to do with each other. She didn't want to play. You do. That's life."

I pick up the nutrient guide on the table and turn it over and over.

"She couldn't play," I say. "Even if she says she didn't want to, she might have changed her mind. But she had me."

"I think," says Sophie, "she decided you were more important than tennis. I think even if your mum *had* still loved tennis, she might have given it up. For a while anyway. She had something in life that was a lot more important and wonderful. She had you. A frame with strings and a rubber ball meant nothing compared to a baby. That's how I see it. And I think once she sees you hit a ball, she'll want you to play, Gemma, I really do."

I shrug. "She did say this morning that I should be playing."

Sophie nods. "It's up to you but you're good, Gem. If you love it, then you should play. We only live once. We should do the things we enjoy. You know," she says, tucking her hair behind her ears, "Chris wanted to do so many things. He wanted to visit Nepal and see the Northern Lights. He wanted to take Bradley skiing, and fishing in the Canadian lakes. He never got to do any of it."

She sits back and smiles.

"I hope you don't mind me saying it, but I often wonder what Chris would say. And Chris would say, *Get on that court and blast that ball and give young Bradley a run for his money. He can get a bit cocky sometimes!*"

"He has some awesome shots," I say. "His forehand is a killer."

Sophie smiles at that. "He loves it. Things can be tough for Bradley."

I nod and push my glass away "I'm sorry you had to miss your meeting."

Sophie tips her head back and laughs, very loud. "I'm not! Fussiest client ever, wanting the house to look like a palace for no money at all. I wish I hadn't taken the job!"

"Our flat is tiny, me and Mum's."

"Tiny can be the best," says Sophie. "What's it like?"

So I tell her about the way Mum puts pictures all jammed together on the wall and how the saucepans hang from hooks and how you can only shut the bathroom door once you've wiggled round the other side. And how my bedroom window overlooks the street outside and the street lights cast this golden glow over everything. And how when the big buses go by fast, my windows shake.

And then I really miss Mum and home and I cry a little and Sophie pulls me towards her. Her soft curls fall on my cheek.

"What would you like to do now, Gem?" she asks.

I shrug. I think about Flori and Sarah and how I'm not there.

"How about going back to the club?" she asks, as if reading my mind. "We can swing by Joe's house and I can make you a packed lunch and pick up your things."

"OK," I say. We head back to the car and drive to Joe's and I go upstairs to get ready. My kit's not there and I remember we washed it all last night. It will be soaking wet. I go down to the utility room and open the machine but it's empty. I stand up and there, on the counter, is my kit, neatly folded and ready to be used. Joe must have sorted it all last night. I don't know why but it makes me cry again, the fact he had thought about what I'd need, got everything ready and then I was such a pain and he didn't mind at all. I wipe the tears away, run back upstairs and change. And then I get the little notebook, the one with the tally chart. I open it up and rip out the tally page and screw it into a ball and stuff it in my bag. I would never want Joe to see it.

When I come back down, the lounge door is open. Sophie is looking around the room. I think she might be checking that Lexi's pink mules and tissue boxes are gone, which they are.

Chapter Forty-nine

I hit on the practice wall while they finish up the morning drills. I hit the ball hard, over and over, loving the feeling, ignoring my blisters.

"You're back!" shouts Sarah. "Fab!"

They stop for lunch and I fetch my food. There is a tub of strawberries, a couple of sandwiches and a chocolate bar, and it makes me smile because for the first time my lunch is actually not super giant size.

The sun is shining now. We sit outside, me, Flori and Sarah, on the long wooden bench by court one. All the boys are inside and Minxie is leaning against the netting, her headphones on, a sketch pad resting on her bent knees. She draws and shades, her head twisting from side to side as she makes each new line. She seems just the same. I wonder how she feels about Joe and Lexi not being together any more. Maybe she doesn't know.

Sarah has a boiled egg. It smells really strong.

"That is gross," says Flori. I think she means Sarah's egg so I keep quiet but then I look over and Flori's yoghurt has exploded all over her sandwiches.

"Really gross!" says Sarah.

I hand Flori one of my sandwiches and a few strawberries.

"That's so kind," she says. "Are you sure?"

I nod.

"Why weren't you here this morning?" asks Sarah.

I bite into my ham and cheese sandwich. Sophie has put a thin line of pickle on the bread. It's really yum. I want to say "Oh, my dog had puppies" or "I had to see the dentist and have a filling" but I'm sick of lies.

"Well, let's see." I finish my mouthful, lick my lips. "I thought I had found something out about my dad but it turns out I still know nothing. Like zip. Not where he lives, what he does, whether he has blue eyes or a limp." I can feel the two girls have stopped eating and are staring at their food. "But I did find out something really *big* about my mum and I thought I knew her *really* well." Flori bites into a strawberry and looks at me sideways.

"So that's kind of why I wasn't here."

There is silence, we all keep chewing and then Sarah looks at me and I look at Flori and the three of us start giggling. Real, proper, can't stop giggles. Sarah spurts hard-boiled egg on to the grass. One bit flies across and lands on Minxie's right trainer. Minxie doesn't notice which makes our giggles worse.

Flori has to stand up and gasp deeply.

"Oh, Gemma, I'm so sorry," she says, wiping her mouth, pushing her headband off her forehead. "It beats my sandwich crisis." That sets us off again. Hysterical giggles. And this time Minxie *does* notice but rather than joining in, she mutters something about us being immature, stands up and walks away, the large lump of boiled egg still nestled in the laces of her right trainer.

"She *scrambled* to her feet," says Sarah, in a quiet voice, which sets us off again. I look round to see if Minxie has heard but she has gone inside the clubhouse, which I'm glad about.

"Well, we did *fry* to tell her," says Flori. Sarah laughs so much she falls off the bench. I'm laughing but I feel a bit odd laughing about Minxie. I kind of feel a bit sorry for her. I don't quite know why, but I do.

"I'm just going to the loo," I say, getting to my feet.

Minxie's at the table, sketching, headphones on. She looks up and I smile at her and she makes a little movement with her mouth. Not a smile but a tiny, small something that isn't mean or moody but actually OK.

We spend the afternoon on approach shots and volleys. You hit a short ball and then run in, do a split step and hit it before it bounces. Flori keeps forgetting to run. She misses most of the forehands and then we all yell, "RUN," and she trots into the net and leans on it when she gets there. It makes us laugh so much. It even makes Pam laugh.

"You can't touch the net, Flori!" she shouts.

"It helps me stop!" says Flori. Even Minxie laughs at that.

It feels good to hit the ball. This is my racket and my tennis camp and I love it.

"Good stuff, Gemma!" shouts Pam as I bang a high volley down the line.

"Must be in my blood, hey, Mum," I say but only to myself, just quietly, so only I can hear.

———————

Joe picks me up. "You OK?" he says and I nod because

I am. "I'm glad you decided to get back on court this afternoon."

As I get in the car, Joe's mobile rings. He answers it and chats and then covers the phone so the person can't hear.

"It's Flori's mum. She's not picking Flori up today but she got my number from Sophie. It's Flori's birthday on Wednesday. She wants to take you and Sarah out for pizza and a look round the shopping centre after tennis. Want to go?" I nod hard and sit back and start to get the giggles again just thinking about the flying boiled egg.

Surinder: I'm sock free yippee!!!!

Jess: cool! hows the tennis Gem?

Gemma: great!!! Turns out my Mum used to play.

Jess: cool

Gemma: She was in the under 17 national team and she NEVER told me! Can you believe that? Been a bit odd finding this out.

Jess: OMG I bet

Surinder: I've found out I hate camping and I hate verrucas

Jess: Oh Sinda stop it. Why didn't she tell u Gem?

Gemma: It's a long story. I'll tell you more when I see u. She had me and stopped playing.

Jess: I bet. babies are hard work.

Surinder: my baby cousin is an absolute pain really smells and screams non stop

Jess: 🙈

Chapter
Fifty

Sometimes the tennis feels like it's getting easier, then it feels impossible again. My blisters are bad on my hands and feet. We start today with lots of warm-up runs and hitting forehands, then running in for volleys. It's hot today, the hottest day so far.

"I hope you can both come tomorrow," says Flori as we fill our water bottles. "I did tell my mum that you're probably both busy and would find it ... you know ... not such a great idea."

"OMG," says Sarah, nudging Flori. "I'm so excited! It'll be such fun."

"Yeah, me too," I say and Flori smiles at us both and her shoulders slump a little and she rolls her eyes as if she's totally relieved. I like Flori.

Pam lets me hit with Sarah today and she's so good

that I have to chase and concentrate really hard.

"Have you really *just* started playing?" says Sarah when we stop to collect the balls.

"Yep," I say.

"Wow," she says. She doesn't say anything else. I want to tell her about my mum being a junior champion but it doesn't feel right. *I've* only just found out so it seems odd that I should suddenly tell Sarah.

We practise volleys. Pam feeds lots of balls from her big wire basket.

"One volley and then one smash!" she says, and she asks Sarah to help her demonstrate. The ball goes low for the volley and then high in the air and Sarah smashes it down. It's such fun. We all laugh a lot. Raj hits the ball so hard it bangs against the back netting. Finlay keeps running back and letting it bounce. Minxie and Sarah are brilliant. Flori misses every single ball, flinging her racket through the air, like she's swatting at flies.

"Lobs next," says Pam. "Anyone know what a lob is?"

I want to yell, "I do, I do. My mum was amazing at them." But of course I don't.

Raj throws his hand up like we are at school. "It's when you hit the ball high over the head of your opponent at the net and they can't get it.'

"If it's a bad lob, they can smash it," says Sarah, fiddling with the strings on her racket.

"Excellent," says Pam. She shows us how to lob, how to try to use topspin to send it in a loop. She demonstrates with Minxie. We all have a go. It's hard to judge how hard to hit it so it doesn't go out. The twins keep running back and heading it, like it's a football. One lands on Finlay's nose and he runs off to the clubhouse screeching that it's bleeding and he's going to die and it's all Max's fault.

I scoop the ball high. It sails over Flori's head and she spins under it, wrinkling her nose and watching it like it's a pretty bird in the sky. I sail another over Sarah's head. She jumps to reach it. It just touches the tip of her racket but it goes over her head and lands at the back of the court.

"That's a perfect lob," says Pam. I turn and look at her and she gives me a thumbs up. I want to ask her if she saw my mum lob, if she knows my mum was really good at that shot. But instead, I wait for Minxie to tie her laces and I get the balls ready to feed to her and I bounce them on the ground, over and over, thinking about my mum.

Chapter
Fifty-one

"Targets today!" calls Pam, laying out little multicoloured cones. "I want you to really think where the ball is going."

"Where it's *going*?" says Flori. "I can't even *hit* it!" She straightens the big badge on her T-shirt. It says *12 TODAY* in red letters.

"It may be your birthday, Flori," says Pam. "But you can't leave until you've hit one target. Just one."

"But I brought cakes for lunch, with double icing. Doesn't that let me off?"

"No!" yells Pam and we all laugh.

We serve at the cones. We hit forehands and volleys cross-court and down the line. When one gets hit, everyone cheers and we get a point. Sarah serves hard and sends them flying across the court. Bradley volleys straight at the cones so they spin away. By the afternoon,

Flori still hasn't hit one.

"I'm too full of cake," she says.

Cars start arriving to pick up. Pam stops everyone. She gathers all the cones in one corner of the service box.

"Right, Flori, here we go." She feeds her ball after ball and at last Flori hits the giant target and we all shriek, even Pam.

Flori's mum calls to us from the clubhouse. She is wearing a long red pleated skirt, with a purple net scarf wrapped around her shoulders. She reminds me of Mum in her kaftan.

"Ready, girls?" she shouts. She is nothing like Flori. She is so noisy and her arms move all the time while she talks, pointing and waving.

Sophie pulls up and gets out of her car and walks over to Flori's mum. They chat for a bit and Sophie points at me, and I hear her say, "Just wanted to check you were OK to take Gemma still."

"Absolutely!" says Flori's mum. "It's so great Flori's made such lovely friends. We're going to have tons of fun. We just need Sarah. I haven't met her yet. She looks up and waves madly. "That must be her there. Sarah! Hi! Ready for an afternoon of shopping and pizza?"

We spin round to see who she's waving at. It isn't Sarah. It's Minxie. She is walking to Lexi's car, her headphones on.

"Actually, that's not..." says Sophie but Flori's mum is off, sweeping the net scarf over her shoulder and running over to Minxie, her skirt billowing in the breeze.

Flori looks a little desperate. "What is she *doing*?" she says. She runs over and tries to pull her mum back but she's already talking to Lexi, arms pointing over to us all and to her car, her eyes wide and excited.

"Ooh, she absolutely *must* come!" she shrieks. "Mustn't she, Flori!"

Flori nods as if her head is super stiff and before we know it, Minxie is ambling over to join us.

"Apparently," she says, in a flat voice, all low and cross, "I *absolutely* must come..."

Sarah joins us. "I'm ready!" she says. She has changed into jeans and a T-shirt that says *Keep calm, play tennis*. Her hair is down and frizzy and she has some lip gloss on. I feel stupid for not bringing a change of clothes.

"Great," says Flori's mum, rushing back to join us. "You must be Sarah and isn't it great Minxie can join us too!" We nod and smile in the kind of way you smile at a teacher who says they'll give you extra help with long division at break.

Flori's mum is funny in a good way. In the car she hands out deodorants and mints and snacks. "Thought you'd like to freshen up!" she says.

Flori passes them back from the front seat, her eyes rolling in a sort of "this is what my mum's always like" way.

Everyone says no to the deodorant so I feel I have to as well but I keep it on my lap and hope I can sneak it in my bag somehow and use it later.

The car is old and it squeaks. There are dog hairs everywhere and the seats have big holes in them. Minxie shifts as far into the corner as she can to avoid sitting on a large sticky patch. I'm in the middle. There is an old magazine on the floor so I put it over the patch and give Minxie a very tiny smile.

"Thanks," she says and she stares at the front cover. It's a movie star wearing a black dress with safety pins down the side. "That's an iconic look," she says and I smile again and nod but I don't know what she means.

We drive a few more miles and pull into a big shopping centre. It's the same one with the sports shop and the cinema.

Flori's mum parks the car. "Now here's the deal," she says. "This is all thanks to Flori's grandma who wanted to spoil you all."

The deal is good. She takes us to a huge clothes shop. She passes each of us a crisp note to spend. "I'm going to sit just there on that big sofa and leave you girls to it!" She walks over to the sofa, the purple net scarf floating behind her. We watch her collapse on to the cushions, sit back and close her eyes, her red skirt spreading out like a fan, her black boots sticking out like doorstops.

The shop is on three floors. I have never seen such an amazing selection of clothes and jewellery and bags.

Flori stands by a rack of belts, staring at the aisles a bit like she stares at a tennis court. "This was Mum's idea," she says. "She thinks it's every girl's dream. I'd rather have taken Gran's money to the bookshop." She looks at us, worried. "I hope you all think it's fun."

Sarah doesn't hear. She's at the hat stand, trying on a baseball cap. I nod but Minxie is spinning round, gazing at the racks of clothes, looking up at the escalator to the floor above.

"This is brilliant!" says Minxie. "Your mum is cool!" She holds up her note. "We can get some really cute stuff with this!"

"Really?" says Flori. She perks up. It's odd but we both do. Minxie being pleased seems to make it more exciting.

"I'll help you," says Minxie. "What's your favourite thing to wear?"

"This," says Flori, tugging on her fleece.

"Oh, honestly!" huffs Minxie and she takes Flori by the arm and marches her round the store, pulling things off the racks and throwing them on to Flori like she is a shopping trolley.

Sarah and I follow, picking up the clothes that Flori drops and listening as Minxie talks through the rules of fashion. Skirt lengths, what to wear with boots, how to layer up under a jacket. It seems like she knows it all.

"That's a start," she says, when we have finished on the first floor. "Let's try them on!"

"I have to try *all* this on?" says Flori.

"All of it!" says Minxie. "But not that." She pulls a grey cardigan from the pile.

"But that's the one thing I chose!" says Flori.

"And that's why..." says Minxie, guiding her into the changing room, "you're not trying it on." She passes her two things. "That top first, with the skirt."

An hour later, we all have a new top or skirt or bag. Minxie found a dress on the bargain rail, a denim dress that looks amazing on her.

"Thanks so much," says Flori, looking up at Minxie. She fiddles with her headband, "I'm really glad you came."

Minxie nods and shrugs and we find Flori's mum and head off to the pizza place.

"You're good at that," I say to Minxie as we wait for the table. "You know, putting outfits together."

"It's what I want to do," says Minxie. "Fashion design, retail. I love it."

"I think you'd be brilliant at it," I say.

"Thanks."

It's the first nice conversation Minxie and I have shared.

We sit down in the pizza place and order our food and then empty our shopping bags and show Flori's mum what we bought. Flori holds up her beaded top and leggings.

"This is my best birthday *ever*!" she says and we toast her with our sodas. The clothes are perfect for Flori. Simple but pretty.

"And don't tuck the top in like you tried to…" says

Minxie. "It's meant to hang over the waistline."

"OK! OK!" says Flori. She shoves the clothes back in the bag.

Minxie puts down her drink and grabs the bag. "You have to take care of your clothes, Flori," she says. "Like you would take care of a book." She takes out the items and folds them neatly, tucking the arms under. She slides them back in the bag, passes it back.

"Thanks," says Flori, staring at her. "I will take care of them." She looks at Minxie and Minxie nods a little and glances at her phone. Flori sits back and sighs, reaches for her lemonade. "It's been such fun and all because of a wretched tennis camp!"

"Floorrri," says her mum in a slow kind of "stop it" voice.

"What?" says Flori, stirring her drink with a straw. "Let's face it, Mum. I'm hardly made for tennis. I'm the most hopeless player in history."

It's hard not to laugh.

"You're not!" says Sarah. "You've improved so much."

"I haven't improved at all. Not one bit!" says Flori. "Oh no! Wait, I have actually. Last week, I hit *myself* with the racket. At least now I can hit the ball and not my knee."

The waitress arrives with pizzas and salad.

"Well," says Minxie, taking a slice of pepperoni. "I've been playing tennis since I was five and I think I stopped improving about three years ago." We are quiet for a moment. And then Minxie says, "So beat that one, Flori!" and we all laugh and it feels good.

Sarah holds her fork up. It has a piece of hard-boiled egg on it. She gives me and Flori a little smile, trying to remind us of the egg thing. But I don't feel like laughing, so I reach for more pizza.

The ice creams come in tall glasses with wafer biscuits. Minxie stirs the chocolate sauce into her ice cream. I stir my raspberry ripple, watching as the colours mix, as the red sauce filters through the vanilla. It's like the red streak is the past, the secrets and the trouble and now it's all stirred in, spread through everything, melting away. I hope that's how the future will be. Soft and pink like the ice cream is now.

I turn a little towards Minxie. "I know the truth, about my mum."

She stops stirring, tilts her head, lifts her spoon out of the glass. "Oh," she says. We are quiet for a moment and then she says, "I don't know much but she sounds pretty cool. She was this superstar and she didn't tell you."

I take a mouthful and nod. "She didn't want to play any more."

"I get that," says Minxie and I smile a little, surprised. It's like Minxie understands this more than anyone else. It's similar I suppose, the way her dad piles on the pressure, pays for the coaching and wants her to be brilliant. But my mum *was* brilliant.

"Does your mum play?" I ask.

Minxie makes a face. "No way! She hates tennis." She digs her spoon into the bottom of the glass. "My dad plays. And Joe plays, of course." She sniffs and tosses her hair over her shoulder, as if she remembers Joe isn't really a part of her life now. I wonder if I should say something about Lexi and Joe not being together but she gets her phone out and I can tell she doesn't want to talk any more.

Chapter
Fifty-two

It rains. It rains so hard that the courts have giant puddles.

"Only two mornings left," says Sarah, standing on the deck, looking out at the courts. "And it's pouring. Really not fair."

"This week has flown by," I say.

"Thank goodness," says Flori. She spins round to look at us both. "We *will* keep in touch though, won't we?"

We both nod.

"Of *course*," says Sarah. "Why don't we all sign up next year for the camp, back here with Pam?"

"Yes, great," I say. "I'll ask Joe if I can stay again."

Flori wrinkles her nose and says, "Maybe."

We spend the morning in the clubhouse. Pam shows us a video on her laptop about hitting a second serve and another one on scoring the games. It's a bit easy for the ones who can play and too complicated for the beginners. Minxie sits at the back, her legs up on the bench, sketching. The twins ask if we can watch Spongebob instead. Raj has his phone under the table and him and Bradley play a game. Flori gets out her book. Sarah yawns a lot. I feel sorry for Pam. I ask a few questions but it makes the others annoyed because she pauses the film each time and says things like:

Now can everyone look this way...

Great point, let me explain...

Can anyone else answer...

There was a famous match at the US Open when...

The rain falls heavier so Pam decides we can go home. We are watching the last film called *Best Volley Tactics* when Sophie arrives to pick me and Bradley up. I wave at her and she raises her hand and stands at the back, watching. When the film is done, I glance round and she is staring over Minxie's shoulder, looking at her drawings.

"These are good," she says to her. Minxie flicks round. She didn't know Sophie was there. "Can I take a closer look?"

Minxie shrugs and nods and Sophie sits down next to her.

Pam talks about the tournament the next day. I don't

really want to play. I'm not ready. I can't serve properly or keep the score.

"Just a bit of fun on the last day," says Pam.

We get up to leave. I watch Sophie slide the sketch pad back to Minxie. They chat for a while and Minxie flicks back through the pages to show Sophie something. And then Lexi arrives, beeping her car horn loudly and Minxie gathers her things and runs out.

We drive home in the drizzle. The tunnel of trees seems heavy in the wet weather. The train tracks gleam as if the rain has painted them silver.

"Joe rang," says Sophie. "He's booked us an indoor court for later, so we can all play."

"Wicked," says Bradley.

"You can play tennis *indoors*?" I say, staring at Sophie.

"It's the best," says Bradley. "It's like carpet."

"OK." I laugh. "I'll give it a go."

We pull on to the drive.

"Did the kittens arrive?" I ask.

"No," says Sophie. "It's good news, though. They were old enough to find new homes and they've all been snapped up."

Bobby is by the front door, hiding under the porch. The rain is heavy again now, bouncing off the roof of the car.

We scuttle inside and make pancakes and cover them in maple syrup.

They call the indoor court the "bubble". The ball echoes and if you hit it really high, it hits the roof and pings back down. Sophie and Joe hit the ball hard to each other, over and over. When Bradley goes to the loo, I watch them play and I think of Mum and how she must have hit it like that. Probably harder and better and further.

When we all hit together, they hit the ball softly for us. I'm glad but Bradley hates it.

"Don't do that!" he yells, glaring at his mum.

"What?" she shouts.

"That thing where you hit it to me like I'm six and I've never played before."

Joe hits with him. He hits it just like Sophie but Bradley returns it without complaining.

We stop for a drink and Mum phones for a chat.

She tells me about a market they went to and how the weather is baking hot. I tell her about the indoor court and how Bradley hit the roof and she laughs and tells me to have fun. We don't talk about the fallout or my dad or the big stuff and I'm glad. I think we both need a break from it. Things are normal again between us and it is such a relief.

I go back on court with Joe. Just me and him on one court. We hit it over and over. Joe gets it back to me in the right place every time. He gives me tips on the grip, how to hit topspin. He feeds me volleys, over and over. I dive and run and hardly miss one, then he comes up to the net and I move back, and I try to give Joe volleys and then he says, "Try a lob," and I loop the ball high over his head, right into the far corner. He runs back but he can't get it. And then he looks at me and smiles and I smile back and I know we are both thinking about Mum.

We drive home with the rain still a faint drizzle, piano music playing in the car.

"Bit naughty," says Joe, "but shall we get a drive-through burger?"

"Yes," screeches Bradley.

"You've done it now," says Sophie.

Joe smiles and we drive to the big shopping centre and wait in the line of cars. Joe and Sophie talk a little, plan the next few days.

"Really sorry," says Joe, turning round to look at me. "I'll be late for the tournament tomorrow. I might only catch the last games."

"That's OK," I say but deep down I'm a little disappointed.

"That's rubbish," says Bradley.

"Sorry, Brad," says Joe. "But I'll try my best to get there."

We drive slowly past the big menu screen. There is so much to choose from.

"And Gem," says Joe. "Thought we'd go straight to Gran's after the tournament. Would that be OK? Pack tonight?"

I nod hard, excited to see Gran and the dogs again.

We pull up at the order window. The girl looks at the car, peers from under her cap.

"Hey, guys! We have some *great* family offers." She starts talking very fast, going through burgers, chips, fries, onion rings, kids' treats. And then she stops and waits and all four of us are very quiet.

"Um," says Joe. "I suppose the big bucket deal?" He turns and looks at each of us.

Bradley is staring at the window of the takeout kiosk. "Do you need to be a family for it?" he says.

Sophie turns round and holds his hand.

"No," says Joe. "Of course not."

"We could pretend," says Bradley. "If it gets us more food."

Everyone laughs at this.

"Great idea," says Sophie. "I think we make an incredible family."

"Too right," says Joe. "We are totally smashing this family thing!"

Sophie laughs and Bradley smiles. I think of Mum.

"Can I have a double patty?" says Bradley.

"You can have anything you want," says Joe.

"Your dad is the *best*," says the girl in the booth and she turns away to the screen and Joe orders the giant bucket and double patty burgers.

We drive away with a huge carrier bag, the car smelling of fried food.

Joe changes the music to a track we know and tells us we have to sing, and we all bellow out the tune, even Bradley, all of us singing so hard that the lorry driver in the next lane hears us and beeps his horn.

Chapter Fifty-three

"Friday tournament! Yeah!" calls Pam as we gather in the morning sunshine. "Team photo first."

I stand with Flori, Sarah and Minxie in front of the clubhouse. Raj and Bradley kneel in front of us and Max and Finlay hold tennis rackets in a cross. For once, they don't argue.

"Let's just get this over with," says Minxie. She is wearing a new tennis dress. It is floaty and falls in one smooth line.

Raj's family have laid out a picnic blanket on the grass beside the court. His little sister waddles around, throwing paper plates like frisbees. Sophie sits with Flori's mum and Sarah's dad, the three of them chatting away. The twins' childminder Suzie chases the twins with a bottle of sun cream, firing it like a weapon, trying to catch a bit of skin. Lexi stays in her car, her music playing softly through the open window.

We start with a round robin. Everyone plays the best of five games against everyone else. So you can win 3–0 or 3–2 or 3–1.

My blisters are bad. Joe has taped them for me but every time I hit the ball, the tape just seems to rub at the broken skin. I think of Mum all those years ago, playing hour after hour, training day after day, and I wonder if she had blisters.

Minxie beats me easily. I beat the twins and Flori, but Raj just pips me 3–2 and Bradley beats me 3–1.

Sarah and I have some good rallies but she's so much better than me. I lose 3–1. We shake hands and then wait for the twins to finish. They are on the next court, playing each other, arguing between every point.

That was in.

No, it wasn't.

You're lying.

No, I'm not.

Yes, you are.

I'm not serving if you make that face.

This is my normal face.

It's a stupid face.

In the end Pam has to go on court and be the umpire. No one really knows who wins in the end, even Pam.

"Right, final game is between Bradley and Minxie," calls Pam. "They won the most games. One full set. The winner wins the day!"

We all cheer and clap. Minxie turns to Pam. "Are you sure it's me?" she says, slumping on to the grass. "I'm sure Sarah won more games than me." Pam tallies up again.

"It's you, Minxie. Look, your dad's just arrived. He'll be thrilled." She puts her clipboard down and disappears into the clubhouse.

"You made the final, Minx?" shouts her dad, striding over towards us. She nods, picking at the clumps of grass. "Great stuff. Let's have the trophy this year."

Everyone is quiet. Even the twins are still, Minxie's father towering over them like a heavy cloud.

Minxie drags herself on court. I wish Jake was there so at least she would try. She makes loads of mistakes. She makes so many that we all want her to get better, hit the ball in, make it a good game.

Her dad glares at the court, both hands shoved in his trouser pockets, jangling his loose change. Lexi gets out of her car and stands in the far corner, well away from everyone, her arms folded. I feel a bit sorry for her.

I wonder if I should go and have a chat. But I'm not sure what I would say.

Bradley wins the first two games and then Minxie comes back. It keeps going like that, Bradley stretching ahead, Minxie catching up.

Bradley goes 5–4 up. One more game to win. Joe arrives and joins us to watch. Bradley sees him and they share a quick thumbs up.

Minxie hits everything else either out or in the net. The match is over. They shake hands and Bradley runs round the court whooping.

"Rotten luck, Minx," says her dad. "Some dodgy line calls there."

Minxie throws her racket down. "No, there weren't any bad calls," she says. "He was the better player. I lost because I wasn't as good and I don't want any more coaching and I don't want to play in any more tournaments."

She stomps into the clubhouse and her dad spins round and walks back to his car, the wheels squealing as he drives away.

Pam presents Bradley with the trophy. She calls Minxie out to get her second prize medal. Minxie tries to smile and then she goes back inside.

"Such a great game," says Pam. "I want everyone to keep playing and hopefully I'll see you *all* next year!" She looks at me and I nod.

Flori and Sarah and I swap phone numbers. Raj gives me his too and tells me he'd like a game with us all.

I look round and see Minxie, sitting on her own in the clubhouse. Pam passes round a plate of cakes so I take two and go inside.

I pass Minxie a chocolate cupcake.

"Thanks."

"Are you OK?"

"Yep." She picks at the cake, peels off the wrapper, wipes her eye fast. I bite into mine and we sit for a minute, just quietly eating.

"It must be hard," I say. "With your dad being so ... keen." I wonder if this is how Mum felt when she didn't want to play. I wonder how many tears she wiped away.

Minxie lines up the crumbs that have fallen on the table.

"I don't want to play any more," she says. "He needs to get it."

"Ooh, I think he did this afternoon." She smiles at that, fiddles with the edge of her sketch pad.

"Can I see?" I ask.

Minxie nods and slides it over to me and folds her arms, lays her head down on them but tilts it so she can watch. I open the first page. They are designs for long evening dresses. One has a slit right up to the thigh and little jewels across one shoulder seam. Other pages have jackets and evening tops. Guys beachwear. Handbags, hats, scarves.

"These are incredible," I say.

Sophie joins us. She walks over and hooks her sunglasses on her head, leans over to see what I'm looking at. "She's talented, isn't she?"

"Very," I say.

Minxie sits up a little, picks at her nails.

"I'd love to help you, Minxie," says Sophie. "I have a friend who's a designer. We were at uni together."

Minxie shrugs.

Lexi comes to the door, rattles her keys. "Minx, let's go," she says.

Minxie gathers her things quickly, shoving the sketch pad in her bag. They turn to leave and Sophie says, "Lexi, can I just say something?"

Lexi turns round, folds her arms and tilts her head as if she can't quite imagine what Sophie might have to say to her.

"Minxie has such a talent for design," says Sophie.

"I've seen her drawings and her passion." Lexi says nothing. "When she's a little older, I could ask my friend who's a fashion designer to give her a few weeks' work experience."

They stare at each other.

Minxie looks at me and raises her eyebrows and makes a funny smirk as if to say "this is interesting ... how's this going to go?".

Lexi says nothing but she nods gently, puts her arm round Minxie and leads her away.

I watch Minxie get into the car and put on her headphones. The car turns and she looks up and gives a little wave and I wave back and I feel strangely sorry that I might never see her again.

Surinder: u can both make my party yes?

Gemma: def yes.

Jess: def yes get back from dads soon

Surinder: going to have nail stuff and BBQ. sound good?

Jess: Great!!!!!

Surinder: shall I ask Nicola? 🤔

Jess: up to u. She wasn't very nice on the residential.

Surinder: that's what I thought and she didn't ask u to her party Gemma did she?

Gemma: that doesn't matter

Jess: I'm going to miss the puppy so much

Gemma: I'm going to miss Uncle Joe

Chapter
Fifty-four

"I'm so glad you were able to stay for a couple of extra nights, Gem," says Gran. She picks up her cup of tea, wraps both hands around it. "Real bonus for me after such a lovely weekend with you and Joe."

I nod. "It's been lovely," I say. And it was. Just me, Joe and Gran at Orchard House. We had driven here straight from the tournament, arriving to excited dogs and Gran fast asleep with the TV on. We'd spent the weekend watching old movies, playing cards, driving Gran round the country lanes and playing tennis at the club. Gran had sat in a comfy deckchair, wrapped in blankets, whooping as we hit the ball. Joe had left us on Monday morning to go to an important work meeting leaving me and Gran for a couple of nights on our own, just us with the carers coming in to help.

"What time is your Mum calling?" asks Gran.

"One," I say, glancing at the clock.

"Same time as my physio," says Gran. "Bossy young thing, she is."

"That's a good thing, Gran."

She smiles and closes her eyes. "I loved watching you play at the club. Those courts look like carpet. I couldn't get over it. Didn't have that in our day. You've learned so fast." She opens her eyes, looks at me. "You're a natural, just like your mum."

"I won't be as good as her," I say.

"You don't know that," says Gran. She puts down her mug. "Anyway, none of that matters. You just *enjoy* it, that's all." She says it quickly, firmly, as if reminding herself of past times, when it mattered too much, and everything fell apart.

"I will, Gran."

I hold her hand for a moment. Copper nudges us both, his nose pushing at Gran's arm. She strokes him and pats him and he nestles next to her. The doorbell rings.

"That'll be that bossy young thing," says Gran, and she twists round and reaches for her frame. "Carers, physios, I *hate* all this fuss."

I go to the front door and let the physio in.

Gran follows her to the lounge, pulling a funny face at the woman's back as if she's being dragged off to the torture chamber.

I sit back down. Mum calls. I press the screen and there she is, sitting in a café. She is so close to me and yet so far away. I don't know why but I'm suddenly a little tearful. She is talking to someone, ordering a drink. There's a doorway behind her and a car passing in the street. Red and white flowers cover the wall in the background. A huge fan hangs from the ceiling above her head, its blades spinning. Everything around her is so not my mum and yet she is there, just the same, hair hitched up, nose now covered in freckles.

"Hey, love," says Mum. "I found the best Wi-Fi café in town. How are you?"

"Yeah, great," I say, fighting the little tear that is still pricking at the corner of my eye.

"Have you had fun, Gem?"

"Yep. So much fun. Joe's coming to collect me later today but I've loved staying with Gran and taking Cooper and Tom for walks. And I'm meeting up with Flori and Sarah and Raj tomorrow to play." I stop there, not sure if she'll like that but she is smiling, nodding.

"What's your favourite shot?" she says.

"Volleys!" I shout. "Love 'em!"

"Got to watch you don't get lobbed," says Mum.

"I know! And I know you were *brilliant* at lobbing!"

She smiles. "Not bad," she says. "So what have you and Joe got planned for the last ten days?"

"We're going away this weekend with Sophie and Bradley, to a hotel with a tree trail and a swimming pool. And then, you'll never guess what... Joe is taking me to *London*!"

Mum sits back, nods slowly. "Gosh, home is going to seem very boring." She fiddles with the hoops on her necklace, twisting them over and over.

I sit forward, get as close to the screen as I can. "Mum, I can't wait to get home. I'm so excited to see you and get back to our flat and see my friends. Surinder's party is right after we return and I've got that swim course, the one with diving."

"Yes, you have."

A waiter puts a drink in front of her and she picks up the little plastic stick and stirs it.

"Have you been on a donkey again?" I ask.

"No! But we did have a salsa lesson," she says. "I was hopeless, couldn't get it at all."

I want to say, "You wouldn't have been if it was tennis,"

but I don't.

She giggles a bit, her mouth lifting just like Joe's does when he smiles.

"Reuben had a right time last night. He thought there was a poisonous spider in his loo. Screamed the whole ship down. You've never seen anything so funny, Gem. Him and Jerry..." she stops there, gasps a little as she laughs, "running down the corridor in their boxer shorts ... with everyone poking their heads out of their cabins to see what the fuss was all about."

I laugh too. "Was it poisonous?"

"No! Just a common harmless one, but massive!"

We talk about the ship and her trips and the things I did with Gran. It's great having time to chat and tell our stories, just me and Mum.

"I passed that last bit of the nursing module, Gem," says Mum. "I had an email from uni yesterday."

"That's great. You're getting closer and closer to being a nurse!"

"Sort of," she says. "Still years to go." She sips her drink. I know how much she wants to be a nurse, how hard it is to fit everything in with work and me and studying. "But it's fine," she says. "It will happen when it's meant to, like most things in life."

We're quiet for a few seconds and then I say, "I have been homesick, Mum, just a little bit, you know."

And she says, "Yes, me too, Gem. I've been Gem-sick."

I laugh at that and then the café door opens behind her and I see Jerry and Reuben and Sadie come in, all with bags of shopping. They come over to the table and say hi and talk very loudly, babbling about the marketplace and the presents they've bought. I'm hoping they will go in a minute, leave us to our call but they sit down at the table and the waiter comes over and they order drinks.

"Better go I suppose, Gem," says Mum. It's odd because the others are bustling around her, loud and busy and yet Mum looks sad and a little alone and I feel the same. "I can't wait to see you. Love you loads."

"Love you more," I say.

"See you in just over a week."

"Yep," I say and I blow her a kiss.

"And Gem," she says, standing up, taking her phone to a different part of the café. "When I get home, we will talk lots and there isn't anything you can't ask me. OK?"

I nod, hard.

"Have a great time with all those fun adventures," she says. "Tell that brother of mine that he's really sort of OK."

"I will. Bye, Mum."

She waves with her free hand and the call ends.

I sit and watch the blank screen for a moment. I'm so pleased she mentioned Joe in that way. "Really sort of OK" is good. A good place to start. Like Mum is melting a little, ready to make amends, to start being a family again.

I can hear Gran laughing with the physio. They come out of the lounge.

"You're doing so well," says the physio, walking towards the door. Gran looks at me, leaning on her frame. She pulls a face as if she's spent the last half hour being dragged over hot coals. The lady turns round and Gran's expression changes to a smile, just in time. "I'll see you Friday."

And then she leaves and Gran looks at me and says, "Help me upstairs to recover, will you, Gem?" and I help her on to her clever magic lift that takes her upstairs. I climb the steps beside it as it travels, Tom following at my feet.

"I pretend I'm sitting up high," says Gran, "crossing snowy plains, about to take to the slopes, my skis dangling from my boots." She lifts her feet up, her fluffy slippers side by side. "Nearly there," she says. It makes me think of Bradley and his dad and how much he wanted to take him skiing.

Gran goes to her room and I go to mine and finish packing my things, ready for Joe when he comes. I lie on the bed and look around the room, at the pictures and the books and the world that Mum once lived in and it reminds me of our call today and the café and how everything around her looked so different and how it is the same here, in this room where she grew up.

I think of me and Mum in our tiny flat where everything makes sense, everything seems to fit. Our home, just me and Mum.

Chapter
Fifty-five

The next week flies by. Joe has time off work. I meet up with Flori and Sarah and Raj at the club. Bradley comes too and we all mix in and play and it's fun. Joe and I watch movies and we go away with Bradley and Sophie for the weekend to a place with an adventure park. The tree-trail is the best bit, hooking on to the ropes up high. Joe hates heights so we have to help him along, guide him through each bit, try not to laugh as he wobbles across the bridges, his eyes shut tight.

We get the train to London, stay in a little apartment, me on a pull-out sofa bed with a massive duvet and piled-high pillows. London is big and hot and busy. I've never seen so many people, heard so many different languages, walked along streets rammed with so many people. Joe holds on to my hand as if I'm six and I clutch it back with absolute relief. His phone number is stuffed in my sock, written on a scrap of paper, just in case we get split up and I lose my phone. We tumble off streets into a quiet café, a garden tucked into a square, a gallery where the atmosphere is beautiful and quiet. And then we are back out again, into the crowds.

"It's magical the city, Gem, isn't it?" I nod and smile. "Like Gran's garden," he says and I nod double speed and he laughs.

We come into a square with a juggler performing on a high wire, shouting out his lines, making the crowds laugh. We stand and watch him for a few minutes and then Joe says, "This is Covent Garden. I want to show you the market, see if we can find you something special." He takes my hand and leads me down an avenue lined with huge white stone pillars.

"I have my ten-pound note," I say and I put my hand in my pocket and check it's still there. Maybe I should stuff it in my sock.

There are stalls with pots and T-shirts and beautiful wooden signs, with cats and dogs painted in the corner.

"They are lovely," I say. "You should get one for your house with Carrot on it!" Joe smiles and says maybe and he takes a photo of the details to order online. We buy ice creams and wander around, watching the people and gazing at the things for sale. We stop at a jewellery stall, silver necklaces laid out with people's names on chains. I point at one that says Carrie and then Joe finds a Gemma one. The letters are slightly slanted but neat, the chain thin and silver.

"You like it?" says Joe.

I nod and pull out my ten-pound note. He puts his hand up to stop me and then he picks up the Gemma necklace and passes it to the man on the stall, taking out his card to pay.

"Would you like to wear it now?" asks Joe, and I nod and he helps me to put it on.

"Thanks," I say, patting the letters around my neck.

He smiles and takes my hand tight and we skip through the crowds, dashing in and out of couples and strollers and families. It makes me think of the airport when I first met Joe, almost four weeks ago, when I followed him through the crowds, when I didn't know him at all, when it would have felt really odd to hold on to his hand.

We come out again on the square. The juggler is finishing his act, announcing his final trick. We stand and watch. He climbs on to a unicycle and juggles, his legs spinning and the balls flying. The crowd cheers. It's like my life in the last four weeks. So much to catch and hold on to and follow. Everything in a spin.

At last, the juggler jumps down, puts the balls safely on the ground in a basket. He brings the basket round and asks for donations, telling funny jokes as he walks among the crowd. Joe rummages in his pocket and passes me a coin.

"Throw it in!" he says and when the juggler passes, I toss it in and he winks at me and says, "Nice one," and I smile back, glimpse the juggling balls nestled in a pile at the bottom of the basket, covered in coins and notes.

Gemma: I've been to London, it was soooo cool 🏰

Jess: I'm so jealous

Surinder: I've been lots of times

Gemma: Oh

Surinder: I've asked Nicola. She can come.

Now I'm not so sure.

Jess: It'll be fine

Gemma: Totally 👍

Chapter Fifty-six

"You must be exhausted, Gem," says Sophie, squirting ketchup on her burger. "Back from London last night, the zoo today. Has Joe let you have *any* down time?"

I laugh and shake my head.

Bradley shoves his chips in fast, as if someone is about to take them away.

Sophie points at my necklace, "That's lovely," she says.

I lift it gently. "Joe bought it for me, in Covent Garden. Have you been?"

"A long time ago," says Sophie.

"There were so many lovely things," I say. "Joe *still* wouldn't let me use my ten-pound note so I'm spending it today, in the gift shop."

Sophie smiles. "You must be so excited to see your mum tomorrow."

I nod. "They've had dolphins following the ship."

"Wonderful," says Sophie.

"Cool," says Bradley.

Joe lays out the map of the zoo and asks what we would like to see next. Bradley leans over, lays his head on Joe's arm and stares at the map.

"Those." He points at the red pandas. A few crumbs from his roll drop on to Joe's arm but Joe doesn't say anything.

"Red pandas, here we come," says Joe and he looks at Sophie and smiles and she leans into him and I just catch his arm wrapped around the back of her waist.

We tidy our table and leave the café. We pass the elephants and watch them for a few minutes. They make me think of the paperweight and Mum and seeing her tomorrow. I've done so many amazing things, met so many exciting people, been to London, had treats I never imagined I would *ever* have. But the thought of just a normal night in our little flat with the buses rumbling by and the arctic desert shower and our tiny kitchen with the pink cupboards makes me feel so happy.

We walk past the chimpanzees and follow the map to reach the red panda enclosure. It looks empty.

"They must be inside their little house," says Sophie.

Bradley gets a bit annoyed and sits down in a grump, waiting. We wait ages. Sophie's phone rings.

"I'll just take this," she says, glancing at Joe. She walks off to a quiet bench under a tree. She talks for quite a while. She looks very serious for a lot of the call.

"Everything OK?" says Joe when she gets back.

"Yes," she says. "Just a cat issue. New one coming."

I walk closer to the fence and then Bradley jumps up.

"Look!" he yells. "They aren't all inside. There's one up in that tree." He points and we follow his gaze and at last we spot it, way up, nestled in a fork of the branches.

"How does he do that?" mutters Joe with a shudder, and we all laugh and tease Joe that he'd be the worst red panda ever.

We spend a lot of time with the okapi and the giraffes. I love the giraffes with their long eyelashes and mottled bodies. We stop for ice creams. Bradley chooses a giant rainbow lollipop.

Sophie shakes her head. "You'll be bouncing off the ceiling with all that sugar."

At the gift shop, I get out my money and buy three key rings. One is an elephant key ring for Mum. I tuck that one in my bag. The other two are giraffes for Joe and Sophie. I give the key rings to them outside the shop and they both put them on their keys immediately, sliding the silver rings in place.

"Thank you," says Sophie and she hugs me hard. "I'll miss you, Gem." She looks at Joe and they don't think I see but I do. I see him stroke her cheek and the way she tilts her head slightly into his hand. And then Bradley screeches very loud. The top of his giant lollipop has snapped off and is on the tarmac.

Chapter Fifty-seven

Joe's car is a bit squashed with me and Bradley in the back but Joe has cleared the seat of tins and rackets. Just one loose tennis ball rolls at my feet. I fall asleep on the way home and wake up to Sophie's voice. She is on her phone.

"We'll be home soon. Yes, just wait there. Thanks."

She hangs up, leans round and taps Bradley on the knee. He's asleep too, the remains of his lolly stuck to his chin. "Wake up, love."

He groans a little and opens his eyes and peels the lollipop free.

"We have a new cat arriving that needs us," says Sophie.

"What, tonight?"

"Yes," she says. "Will you help me settle it in?" He shrugs

and licks the remains of the lolly.

We come off the motorway and after a short while we are in the tunnel of trees. We rumble over the train tracks, follow the road and soon we are outside Sophie's house. A red car is parked on the road. Something about it looks familiar. A lady gets out and smiles at us. I've met her before, I'm sure. Joe parks the car and he gets out with Sophie. Sophie comes round to Bradley's side, opens his door, leans down.

"I've got a surprise for you."

"I don't really want to help with the new cat," says Bradley.

She smiles, strokes his cheek and says, "Oh, I think you'll want to help with this one. What if the new cat is Mungo and he is back to stay and he is yours, just yours?"

Bradley stares at her. He is tired and happy and confused all at the same time.

"Really?" he says.

"Really," says Sophie.

Bradley cries a little, buries himself in her neck and they stay like that for a few moments. I'm not sure if I should get out or just stay very still.

"He won't have to go back again?" he says.

"No," says Sophie. "He's coming to live with us for good."

"I wish Dad could meet Mungo."

"I know," says Sophie and she holds him tight. I jump out of the car and wait with Joe. After a minute Sophie and Bradley join us.

"Thank you so much for this," says the lady.

"Bradley will give him the best life he could have," says Sophie.

The lady looks at Bradley and says, "My mum has to move into a flat to make life easier for her. There is no outside space and no cats allowed. She wondered if you would look after Marmaduke properly, be his owner."

Bradley leans into Sophie and nods hard.

The lady turns back to her car and lifts the cat carrier out. Mungo is staring through the bars. He meows a little and Bradley walks over and kneels down, reaches in and strokes his paw.

"Hi, Mungo," says Bradley and he whizzes round to look at the lady, as if he has done something wrong. "Sorry, I call him Mungo. Is that OK?"

The lady smiles. "I think that's perfect. He's your cat now."

Joe wraps his arm around Sophie. The lady passes Bradley the cat carrier. He takes it and glances at Sophie, smiling. He stops for a second, stares at Joe's hand resting on her shoulder. He doesn't say anything, just leans into her side again and puts his finger through the bars and waits for Mungo to nuzzle it.

Joe points to the doorstep where Bobby is waiting. "Not sure what his lordship will think."

"He'll be just fine," says Sophie and she scoops Bobby up and opens the front door.

Chapter
Fifty-eight

Joe checks his phone. "Looks like the flight's landing on time."

"OK," I say. "Shall I leave my racket here?"

He picks up my bag and puts it in the boot. "No, take it, Gem. Hopefully you'll be able to play again soon." I smile and place the racket on top. Carrot Cake trots past, so I lift him up and stroke him hard.

"I'll miss you, Carrot," I say, nestling into him. "Stay away from that road, little man." He purrs softly and I tickle him under the chin.

"Waste of space," says Joe but he reaches over and runs his hand over his tail. "OK, I think we've got everything."

I pop Carrot inside and Joe closes the door and locks it. I get in the car and put my backpack by my feet, get out my book for the journey. My special people map is there in its plastic folder.

The postman pulls up and Joe chats to him, takes a parcel and a pile of mail. I get out the mind map and a pen. I add Flori and Sarah to the friendship line and link Sophie and Bradley to Joe. And then I draw a big heart right next to Joe's name and Gran's and an even bigger one next to Mum's.

Joe gets in the car. "What's that?" he says, and I show him. He takes it and looks at it and touches the hearts and says, "I'm so lucky to be on there."

"I know," I say, "you are," and we both laugh.

Joe has the parcel with him. He lays it carefully on the back seat, which is covered once again in rackets and balls. When Joe met me at the airport, I had laid his jacket on the same pile. It already seems so long ago. A lifetime ago. I feel like a different person now.

We pull out of the drive and I look back at Joe's house and let out a little sigh.

"You OK?" he says.

"Yep." I look down at my mules. I wanted to wear them. So much has changed but the mules take me back to me and Mum. I think of seeing her and I get a flutter in me. I can't wait.

We drive away. We won't go under the tunnel of trees or across the train tracks. I won't see Sophie and Bradley and Mungo.

We head down the lanes and turn on to the busy main road.

"Excited to see your mum?" asks Joe.

"Very. I just hope that..." He waits while I find the words. "I just hope she wants things to get better as much as me. She did say you were 'sort of OK' so I think that means she does!"

Joe laughs. "I'll take it!" We slow up in a line of cars. "I think it will take time but I can't see her wanting to go back to how things were. No one wants that."

I nod and look out at the fields.

"Joe." I twist my mouth, deciding how to say it.

He glances at me. "Yeah?"

"Can I come again, you know, to stay?"

He glances over at me quickly, smiles that smile that is just like Mum's.

"Reach back," he says, "and open the parcel. It's for you." I twist round and find the brown package on the back seat. "I'm so glad it arrived in time."

I tear the brown card and start ripping off the paper. There is lots of tissue.

"I hope it's OK," he says. "I ordered it from that stall you loved in Covent Garden." He sits up a little, rubs his hands over the steering wheel as if he's a bit nervous, glances over again as I unwrap it. "It's to hang at my house, if that's OK?"

The last piece of tissue pulls away. It's a wooden sign, red with a blue and white checked border and a rope to hang it with. It says *Gemma's room*. In the corner is a little ginger cat, curled up asleep.

"It's perfect," I say and I smile at him and he taps the wheel as if that is good news and he flicks on the radio and turns the music up loud and we sing along because it's a song we both know.

Chapter
Fifty-nine

I lean over the arrivals' barrier, stare down the lane of white polished tiles.

"Ready to see your mum and Jerry," says Joe. "Hand in hand?"

I elbow him hard. People start walking through, pushing trolleys piled high with luggage.

"Bit early yet for your mum's flight," says Joe.

I watch as people dash over and hug their family. One little girl runs across the shiny floor yelling "Grandpa!" An elderly man in a flat cap scoops her up and they join a group gathered under a British Airways sign. It's just like the sign I waited under with Mum, all those weeks ago, waiting for Joe.

So much of my life has changed but everything about the airport is exactly the same; the signs, the clock, the voice announcing flights.

"What's the plan today?" I ask. "Are we getting a taxi or are you driving us home?"

"What would you like to do, Gem?" says Joe.

I stare down at my mules, lift my hands off the rails and rub my fingers over my healed blisters. I look back down at the arrivals' lane but it's quiet now, just a family making their way with bags balanced high.

"I'd like to go to Orchard House," I say. "Just for the night. So we can all be together." Joe nods and smiles as if that sounds a good idea.

The arrivals lane gets busy again. Patterned shirts and shorts, burnt shoulders and sundresses. Suitcases bulging and children crying.

And then she is there. Walking towards me in a huge straw hat, smiling but also crying, her arms outstretched when she sees me, her suitcase abandoned. I run over and bury myself into her, her straw hat falling to the ground.

"I missed you so much," she says. "I'm not leaving you for that long again, Gem." I hug her tight. Everything about her is home, normality, my life.

Joe comes over and scoops up Mum's hat and rescues the suitcase.

"Had a good time?" he says, kissing her on the cheek.

"Yes," she says. She moves her handbag to the other arm and looks at him. "Thanks for taking such good care of Gemma." They stare at each other for a second and Mum twists the silver hoops on her necklace. She is about to say something else when Jerry comes up behind her and puts his arm round her shoulder. He looks as pale as ever with just a little bit of pink on his cheeks. His hair is tied in a big knot at the back.

"We're off," he says. "Hey, Gemma, how are you?" He lets go of Mum and hugs me.

"Jerry," says Mum. "This is my brother Joe." Joe and Jerry shake hands. Joe looks at me and smiles.

And then another man joins us. He is very tall and very handsome.

"This is Reuben," says Mum. "Jerry's partner."

Joe shakes Reuben's hand and I say hi. They chat and laugh and as they walk away, Joe turns to me and says, "Fair play," and I nudge him and say, "Told you."

"So wonderful to see you," says Mum, stroking my hair. Her nose has Caribbean sunshine freckles.

"Yep." We walk together, arms linked, following Joe as he wheels the suitcase back to the car park.

"You OK?" she says, pulling me close.

"I'm great," I say, resting my head on her shoulder. And then I can't help it. "Why didn't you tell me? Why all the secrets?"

She kisses my head, holds me tight and says, "Not here, Gem. Let's get home."

We go through double doors and hit the fresh air and sunshine. Mum breathes it in, tips her head back.

"Oh, the freshness," she says.

Joe stops then, switches Mum's suitcase to the other hand. He looks at Mum, lays his hand gently on her shoulder. "I know you're keen to get home, Carrie, but Gemma would love to spend tonight at Orchard House. All of us together. How would you feel about that?"

"Is that what you want, Gem?" asks Mum.

I nod hard. "Just one night," I say. "And then home tomorrow, you and me."

She hugs me tight, her soft tanned skin wrapped around mine. Then she smiles and says, "Good plan." And she looks at Joe and mouths the words "thank you" and I feel so glad.

We set off again, Joe striding out front, the suitcase banging against the metal barrier.

"Be careful," she shouts. "There's a giant vase in there from Barbados!"

He stops and turns back and stares at her. "How did you fit that in?"

"My kaftan is stuffed inside it!"

"Shame you didn't just leave it there," says Joe and he smiles and turns away again.

"So rude," says Mum.

"But so great," I say.

Chapter Sixty

Mum and Joe chat in the car on the way to Gran's. I'm squashed in the back again. Joe's car is so noisy and rumbly that it's hard to hear but I catch quite a bit, especially when we stop at the lights or get stuck in a traffic jam. They talk about the weather and Gran's health and Joe's job and Mum wanting to be a nurse. And then they talk about me. Mum glances back and I pretend to be asleep, slumped sideways, knees up.

"The tennis camp was naughty," says Mum.

"I know," says Joe. "It was naughty and unfair and brilliant at the same time."

"You forced things when I wasn't ready."

"I'm not sure there ever would have been a perfect time."

Mum sighs. "Maybe not."

"You should see her hit the ball, Carrie. It's you all over again."

They are quiet then and I open my eyes, a little smile on my lips.

Mum doesn't say anything else. She tips her head back against the seat rest. I can't see her but I'm pretty sure she shuts her eyes, to let Joe know she doesn't want to talk any more.

She does that sometimes.

Mum is quiet and a bit tearful at Gran's house. It worries me. She was so happy at the airport.

"Give her a bit of time," says Gran. "She's not been here since the wedding, remember? Just like you. We've wasted so much time. No more, though."

She leans over the sink, takes another plate to wash. She scrubs it hard, looks up and out at the lawn, watches Joe and Mum sitting on the grass, talking.

"Just too much wasted time," she says.

I join her at the sink, take the sponge from her and tell her to sit down. I finish the last plates, piling them up on the draining board.

"It's just the way it had to be," I say. It's odd but I can feel Sophie guiding me, next to me. Sophie made me see things from all sides, made me think a bit differently. "We have some great times ahead."

"Yes, we do!" says Gran, gathering the serviettes into a pile. "You certainly do have a wise head on your shoulders, Gemma. Your mum's done a great job with you."

Joe comes into the kitchen and puts the kettle on. I look up and check Mum is still in the garden. She is back in the straw hat, blowing a dandelion, the white wispy seeds floating across the lawn.

"Yes, she has," I say. I kiss Gran on the cheek and head outside to join Mum. There is something we have to do.

Chapter Sixty-one

We push the gate together. The gardener has trimmed the undergrowth, so it opens easily this time.

"I remembered, you know," I say. "It all came back the first day I was here. I remembered the gate at the wedding, how you didn't want me to open it. How you bought me the doll on the way home."

Mum smiles. "Oh yes, that doll. That was important. You were so desperate to see behind the gate. But I couldn't go there."

"I know."

The court is damp and slippy. Mum gasps a little as we walk around it. She reaches the net and strokes the top, twisting some of the broken threads back into place.

"I spent hours on here as a kid. Hours and hours. Just bashing that ball back and forth. Mum and Dad bought me and Joe a ball machine. You loaded it up with balls and it fed you hits, hour after hour." She twists her necklace, playing with the silver hoops. "Joe and I would be out here, hitting balls until the last of the light was gone. Gran would yell out of that top window up there..." She points up to the highest point of the house. "*Come in! You'll trip!* But we never did – trip, I mean!"

"It must have been fun back then, having Joe as a brother."

Mum looks at me, smiles. "Yes. Especially in those days before ... you know."

I nod. I do know, now.

Mum looks at the court, the house, the lawn. I think the memories are flooding in, good and bad.

"I know all about the fallout now, Mum. How awful it was. Joe told me. He feels really bad about it."

She swings round, turns to face me. "Yes," she says. "We've talked about it."

I nod.

"It was hard, Gem."

"I bet."

"I suppose it was hard for everyone," she says.

I nod. "I love being with Joe."

She laughs, cups my face in her hands.

"Told you, didn't I. I told you that you would love him. Everybody does."

"I just hope, Mum..." I stop, worried I'll upset her.

"What, Gem? Go on..."

"I just hope I can spend time with Joe again, stay with him and Carrot, come and see Gran."

She looks at me and smiles, kisses my forehead.

"And I'd like it even more," I say, "if we can sometimes do that together."

She nods hard, takes my hand. "I think that sounds lovely," she says.

We walk on, round the court. "This all needs cutting back," says Mum, reaching up to the overhanging greenery from the trees at the side of the court.

"I like tennis," I say. "And I'm kind of good at it."

She nods. "I'm glad."

"It feels right," I say. "You know, being there on the court at forty–love down with blisters on your hands, knowing you can do it."

She looks at me. "Yes, that is a good feeling."

"I want to play with you. I want you to show me, teach me."

"Oh, Gem, I haven't played in years."

"But we can play now."

Mum pulls her foot along the painted white line on the court. "Blimey," she says. "Pick up a racket again. Never thought I'd do that."

The sun peeks from behind the clouds. We both turn to it, feel the warmth.

"Look," she says. She points towards the house. A rainbow is overhead. We gaze up, follow the colours.

"It was odd, Mum," I say, both of us still looking at the sky, "when I thought the tennis genes might have been from my dad. It felt odd, thinking about him." Mum drops her head, breathes out gently. "It felt sort of nice too, that I was discovering things. Did he play tennis at all?"

She laughs again, shakes her head. "No!"

"I want to know more about him, Mum. Why didn't..." I stop and fight the urge to cry.

She looks at me. "What, Gem?"

"Why didn't he want to know me?"

She gasps a little then, brings both her hands to her face, stares at me with wide eyes. "Oh, Gem!"

"What?" I ask. "What is it?"

"He doesn't know about you." The words tumble out quickly, falling over each other as if they had been queuing there for years and years, waiting for the time to spill off her lips.

"Oh," I say.

"I didn't find out I was pregnant until I was home, back from America. It just didn't feel right, to involve him then." She stares at me, strokes my cheek. "I don't know if that was the right thing to do or not. The years went by and we were so happy, just the two of us, and it seemed so hard to think about sharing you." She looks away for a second and then back at me. "I'm not sure that was fair." And then she puts her hands behind her neck and undoes the clasp from the silver necklace.

"What are you doing?" I say.

She carefully holds the chain and lets the two silver hoops fall into her hand.

"There were three of them. Three silver hoops. I bought this in America."

I stare at her. She fiddles with the hoops, turns them over, traces the rings. She looks at me and smiles. "We bought it. Me and your dad." She gasps a little, as if saying that word shocks her a little.

She passes me one of the hoops. I undo my Gemma chain and we slip the silver hoop on to it. It settles next to the letter G.

"I like the necklace," says Mum, her fingers gently running over the letters. "Did Joe buy it for you?"

"Yes, in London."

Mum nods, smiles. "Your dad has the third loop."

"I'd like to know more about him," I say.

"I know." She glances around her, scuffs the ground, puts her own chain back on. "Give me a little time to get used to all of this and then we can talk about it." She helps me to put the chain back round my neck, fasten the clasp. "It feels good to finally have things out in the open, Gem, and strangely good to be back here, at the house."

"I'm glad," I say.

"Pretty," she says, gently twisting the "Gemma" into place. "It sits perfectly with it." She lifts her own single hoop, twists it a little as if to see how just one feels. "You have his eyes, Gem. Gorgeous chocolate eyes. And his kind heart." We have a big hug, a huge hug, one of those that almost topples you over.

We hear the gate click and turn to see Joe and Gran slowly walking towards us. Gran is pushing her frame, Joe helping to guide her. The gardener is following, Joe's phone in his hand.

"Forty–love down is tough," says Mum, unwrapping herself from me. "Did you come back and win the game?"

"Course I did," I say, with a smile. "It's in my blood."

We laugh at that and join the others.

"Thought we'd take a photo," says Joe. "You know, the four of us." He is holding a can of balls. "One each, high in the air, just like when your grandpa was here, Gem." He hands out the balls. Mum takes hers slowly, gently, as if it is something fragile. She rolls it round and round in her hands, lets it bounce on the ground, lifts it and smells it, closes her eyes. It must remind her of her old life, before me.

"Just here, I think," says Joe and he checks the sunlight and helps Gran to balance while she throws. The gardener holds up the phone.

"On my count," shouts Joe. "One, two, three!" And we all throw the balls in the air, laughing as they fly above us and then bounce back on to the court. Gran grabs her frame. The gardener passes back the phone and Joe collects the balls.

Mum hugs me tight and whispers very gently in my ear, "Love you so much, Gem."

And I tell her I love her back.

FIVE MONTHS LATER
December 23rd

Chapter Sixty-two

"That's too close." Joe looks in his wing mirror.

"It's fine," says Mum, straightening the steering wheel.

"Are you teaching," says Joe, "or am I?"

Mum ignores him and pulls on the hand brake. I sink down in my seat. Last time she practised parking, Joe insisted she got out and he parked the car and Mum went into a right huff.

"You're getting better at everything except for parking," says Joe.

"I'm brilliant at parking."

"You are so not," says Joe.

"It's this car," says Mum. "It's odd." She looks at him. "Like you."

"Well, it's my car and you're extremely lucky I'm letting you drive it at all."

She smiles at him and says, "I know I am." She takes the keys out and passes them over and I let out a loud sigh.

"Hey," says Mum, turning round. "What's that for? I'm getting really good!"

"I'm just glad we're here," I say and I look out of the window. It's very dark and cold and there is a scattering of snow on the ground. "Where's the church?"

Joe points up a little pathway. "Just up there. I've brought you a torch."

Mum peers out. "Not been here for years," she says.

"I know," says Joe. "You OK?"

"Yep, it's important to Mum."

Joe nods.

"Sophie's coming, right?" says Mum and Joe says, "Yep, dragging Bradley with her." They both laugh and I undo my seat belt.

"Right," says Joe, "I'll go and pick up Gran. Won't be long."

Mum nods and we climb out and Joe comes round to the driver's side.

"When I pass my test," says Mum, "can I have this car?"

"Only if you take Carrot Cake with it," says Joe, and of course I yell yes and mum yells no.

He passes us a big torch and then gets in the driver's seat and waves at us and sets off.

We walk up the path, following the ray of light. There is a family in front of us, all wearing head torches. We have to open a small wooden gate and then we see the church. It looks like a Christmas card, with the snow round the doorway. The entrance is small and dark except for a Christmas tree covered in fairy lights. A lady passes us a piece of paper.

"Welcome to the chapel," she says. "As you know, we are candle-lit. There are torches on the pews if you need them and blankets to keep you warm."

"Thanks," says Mum and we walk in and sit down at the back on a wooden pew. There are other churchgoers scattered around, all huddled in big coats and furry gloves and hats.

"It's so beautiful," says Mum. I nod and sit back and look round at the stained-glass windows and the candles, flickering in their silver holders. Mum takes my hand and wraps hers gently around mine. Music starts from the back of the chapel, gentle classical music.

"I can't believe you're twelve in just a few weeks," says Mum.

I nod, squeeze her hand.

"It's been a good year," says Mum. "Hasn't it, Gem?"

"Yep." I start to say that it's been the best but something stops me. I don't want Mum thinking things are better now, not after all the years she worked so hard to make it good on her own. So instead, I say, "Every year is good, Mum," and she rests her head on my shoulder.

We sit quietly for a few minutes. Mum points at the large nativity set at the front of the church.

"They had that same set when I was your age," she says, leaning into me. "I wonder if the donkey's still there."

"It's chilly," I say, snuggling down in my jacket.

"Very." She glances round at the door again. The lady at the entrance has closed it for a bit, probably to keep the warm air in. The church is quiet and still. The music gently plays.

Mum squeezes my fingers, rubs my knuckles. "I found him, Gem." I turn quickly and look at her. "I've found your dad." She blinks a little, holds my hand tight. "He doesn't know yet, but I've found him and when we decide together that it's the right time, we will contact him."

A shaft of something goes through me. I'm not sure what it is. Excitement, fear, nerves. I loosen my scarf, take off my gloves.

More people come in and find seats. The church is

filling up. They ask if our pew is taken. We say yes and shift our scarves and gloves along the bench to save it for the others. Such a simple, ordinary thing to do when my mum has just told me something extraordinary.

I don't know what to say. I sit back and watch the candles flickering, listen to the music, let this new feeling flood through me.

The vicar comes along and says hello to everyone. She is very smiley. I smile back at her, let a little of my excitement flow out of me. I watch her as she talks to the family in front. And then I put my head on Mum's shoulder and I just say, "Thank you," and Mum says, "Happy Christmas, Gem," and we both smile.

And then I hear Joe's voice, hear Bradley moan about having to leave his game in the car, hear the tap of Gran's stick as she walks towards us. I look up. Sophie is there in her brown hat, her big scarf wrapped tight. She sees me and waves and Mum beckons them all over. We shuffle along the pew to make space. They talk about the snow, the traffic, the candles, the turkey ready to be picked up tomorrow. I'm on the end next to a pillar, the cool of the stone touching my hand.

Mum has found my dad.

We will contact him soon.

The music is a little louder now. Everyone stops talking and settles down in their pew. I look to my right. Joe is there, tucking Gran's blanket around her knees and showing Bradley the hymn sheet with the carols we are going to sing. He looks up, sees me.

"You OK?" he mouths and I give him the thumbs up and he smiles. I wonder if he knows. I think he might.

The vicar moves to the front, looks at us all and the music stops. Mum reaches for my hand. I turn to her and smile and it's funny because as we hold hands, we both reach for our necklaces with our free hand, to twist the little silver hoop that sits around our neck. Mine is tucked next to the letter G, on my Gemma chain that Joe bought me, and I clasp them both very tight, and Mum and I pick up our carol sheets and stand to sing.

Also by Ros Roberts:

"A wonderful tale, told with heart and hope"
– Gill Lewis

DIGGER

HOME IS WHERE

AND

YOUR DOG IS

ME

ROS ROBERTS

Shortlisted for the 2022 Branford Boase Award

James splits his life between his mum's and his dad's houses. It's far from perfect. The one constant is Digger, his dog and best friend. He's the glue that holds the two halves of James's life together.

So when James finds a lump on Digger's leg everything changes. Digger is the one he can talk to about anything. But when it's Digger he needs to talk about, where can he turn?

Nominated for the 2023 Yoto Carnegie Medal for Writing

ROS ROBERTS

EVERY CLOUD

Is Amy's summer OVER before it's even BEGUN?

Amy feels like everything is going wrong when she has to move in with Gran and Pops for the holidays. But when she discovers that kind, quiet Jay from school lives over the road, she realizes that friendship isn't always about who talks the loudest or throws the coolest parties. Sometimes a friend is just someone to talk to. Someone who listens.

It seems like things are looking up for Amy, but when outside pressures start creeping back in, can she hang on to her summer of silver linings?

Acknowledgements

This book is about family, friendship, courage and healing. It has existed in many different guises and years ago, it led me to my wonderful agent Gill McLay. This is our third book together – this book is truly ours and I could only dedicate it to her.

To the team at Little Tiger – once again, it has been the best journey. Jane Harris – your experience and guidance with this story has been such a joy. Lauren Ace, you are always there as a calm, encouraging presence. Charlie Moyler, you are a superstar! Catherine Fortey – the cover is just great! Thank you all so much.

Tennis is a backdrop to Gemma's story but it is an important part of the book and my own life. My parents met on a grass tennis court back in the 1950s. As a family, we all played, and the sport has given us so much. Sitting huddled on a rainy Wimbledon centre court in pre-roof times are some of my happiest memories! The Wimbledon match Joe and Gemma watch is a gentle homage to the great Nadal v Federer final of 2008. Pure magic!

This book is of course, a work of fiction. *But* my brother who I utterly adore, did spend many hilarious hours not letting me go upstairs. Thanks, Al! *And* we do have a cat called Carrot Cake who was run over, rescued and named as such because we were eating carrot cake the day we agreed to take him on. Thanks, Carrot. You are definitely *not* a waste of space.

About the author

Ros Roberts lives in the North of England with her family, two dogs and Carrot Cake the cat. She loves the rain, eating brunch, TV and playing tennis. Ros spent many years working as a primary school teacher and is very happy to be back in the classroom running writing workshops. She has also worked in a ski resort, art gallery, aquarium and at Wimbledon – her favourite place on the planet! *Knowing the Score* is her third book. *Digger and Me* was shortlisted for the Branford Boase Award and *Every Cloud* received a Carnegie nomination.

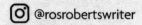

@rosiroberts @rosrobertswriter